Murder in Oregon

They came to the north Oregon coast to live out their
lives in serenity, three women who'd been friends for
decades. Allison's remodeled house in the quaint village of
Windom was a haven for Plum and Jane. They thought
they'd spend their quiet days with music, books, a little
needlework, a bit of gardening, and leisurely strolls along
the beach. They thought they could forget the secret of
murder once done.

But Tommy Weed, a street-smart young punk,
follows them. He knows all about the murder, and plans to
work out his own retirement plan through blackmail.
Overpowering three vulnerable old biddies ought to be a
piece of cake. Age and experience are surely no match for
youth and strength—or are they?

D1601563

Murder Once Done

Mary Lou Bennett

Murder Once Done

A mystery from Perseverance Press
Menlo Park, California

Art direction by Gary Page/Merit Media.
Photography by Rob Egashira/Fabrizio Camera Graphics.
Typography by Jim Cook.

Published by
    Perseverance Press
    P.O. Box 384
    Menlo Park, California 94026

Manufactured in the United States of America.

This book is printed on acid-free paper.

1   2   3   —   90   89   88

Library of Congress Catalog Card Number 87-72896

ISBN: 0-9602676-7-0

*This novel is a work of fiction. Any resemblance to real situations or
places or to actual people, living or dead, is completely coincidental.*

This one's for Ben

"The murder being once done, he is in less fear and more hope that the deed shall not be betrayed or known . . . "

—Thomas More,
Utopia

Murder Once Done

Chapter 1

ALLISON MOFFITT WAS a meticulous strategist, most comfortable when ambiguity was reduced to the manageable. She liked calendars and clocks and pocket notebooks; she liked a bulletin board in the kitchen with bright tacks marching across the bottom ready to rivet timely notices and reminders; she liked a magic marker board on the side of the refrigerator with a felt-tipped pen hanging by a string; she liked a notepad by the phone with a pen in an angled holder, ready to be plucked up and used.

She kept a hefty file folder filled with yellow lined sheets of careful notes about how Crooked House was to operate. She had begun assembling those notes some years ago when it had occurred to her that, statistically at least, she would likely outlive J.P. Moffitt, her fourth husband. While Allison enjoyed living alone some of the time, she had no wish to live out her remaining years by herself; to make a home with either of her two daughters was unthinkable to all three. And so, Allison did as she'd always done: she took charge and made plans. Within six months of J.P.'s demise, she was energetically carrying out those plans which began with the purchase and remodeling of Crooked House on Oregon's north coast and culminated with invitations to two friends to live under its roof with her.

And now it was all about to happen.

In the file folder of notes written on yellow legal paper in her bold handwriting were the rules which would govern Crooked House. Allison had not presented them to her intended housemates as rules, but that's what they were. She

1

understood that the impulse to direct, to manage, to give orders would be irresistible to her; she also understood the reluctance of others to be directed, managed, and ordered about.

It was an experiment, this living together of the three elderly women friends. The selection had been a simple task because Allison had only two friends, Plum and Jane. They'd known each other for over thirty years and, as they were all single now, they would come together to share this house and were likely to be no more miserable than if they were each living alone. At times, the concept filled her with excitement and anticipation; alternately, it sent chills of anxiety rippling through the pit of her stomach. This audacious idea—she did not know if it would take off and soar like the seagulls outside her window or would fall dismally like the spring rains.

Three elderly women living together—what would it be like? They'd all had their own homes, all had their own ways of doing things, all had some experience in living alone to do as they pleased, and were all now uprooting themselves from familiar city surroundings to come to this tiny coastal village where they knew not a soul. What if the ties of friendship were not sufficiently strong to sustain them? What if they fought and squabbled and engaged in endless petty bickering among themselves? It was the day-to-day quality of their life that concerned Allison. The major crises, sickness or death, that might occur—well, she'd observed that people of all ages could generally cope with those big things; it was the small droplets of everyday living that wore down relationships, driving deep wedges that never quite healed, but ground inward, hurtful and irritating.

Allison Moffitt had been an eccentric all her life. Only now, in old age, had she stopped fighting it, stopped denying it, stopped pressuring herself to try to conform.

It is believed that eccentrics are impervious to what others think of their appearance and behavior. For Allison, it had not been so much that she was impervious as that she was

puzzled to realize that the things she wore or did or said were
so at odds with what others expected of her. She could never
quite see why other people regarded her style of dress as
flamboyant when she saw her clothing choices as tasteful and
colorful; it was difficult to understand why her words were
sometimes regarded as unforgivably insensitive while others,
whose words were not so different from hers, were thought
forthright. Now, at seventy-two, she had finally given up the
notion that she was ever likely to untangle this puzzlement.
She felt too old and too tired to attempt conformity. To hell
with it.

Tommy Weed was spawned on the wrong side of the tracks
to a sluttish mother and a father who arrived for seed
planting and departed long before harvest time.

At twenty-five, Tommy believed that the world treated
him with steady disregard, and in this he was correct. Not
much good had ever happened to him, beginning with his
unfortunate physical appearance. He was small, with underdeveloped shoulders and chest; his nose was too long and his
too thin lips covered teeth which crouched inside his mouth
in unpleasant irregularity. But it was Tommy's eyes, deeply
set into his head and the color of old straw, which made
people uneasy, made them want to glance away from him
quickly as though some sinister revelation might seep from
those eyes.

This was a man who sneered in derision whenever he
heard uplifting phrases from the tireless do-gooders who
crossed his path, saying stupid things like "there's enough
love to go around—it's not a scarce commodity." His own
experience was that there was never enough love, never had
been, never would be. There wasn't enough love to give
away to others, and there certainly wasn't enough love to fill
up the empty caverns of his being.

Tommy's philosophy of life was simple: you screwed the
world before it screwed you. That's how you played the
game, how you survived. You looked around and found

somebody weaker, and you took whatever they had that you could use. Or sometimes you just took it because it was there, and the act of grabbing provided a powerful rush that not even cocaine could match.

Tommy had drifted from one menial job to another, never committing himself to the work or the people, chronically complaining and looking for a way to steal from whatever system happened to be supporting him. That was his real occupation: looking for a break, looking for that one moment which would turn his life around and make him happy and loved. It was out there; all he had to do was find it, he was sure of that. He turned his strange yellow eyes on every face he encountered with the unspoken question: are you the one, are you the one who will be my big break and set me up for life?

And when his eyes fell on the old lady, he felt an explosion in his gut that was so powerful it almost made his heart stop. There she was, all right, his ticket to happiness.

She was elderly, she was weak.

And she hid from the world an old and awful secret.

And Tommy Weed knew what that secret was.

Plum was the first of Allison's friends to arrive, brought by one son in a big maroon van, followed by another son driving a fully loaded pick-up truck containing his mother's possessions, securely tied down and modestly draped by a tight tarpaulin as if to shield personal belongings from public scrutiny.

Allison observed their arrival with a pang of alarm. The agreement—drafted on a yellow legal pad, delivered verbally, reinforced in a reminder note on blue stationery—was that Allison would furnish the house, and each woman would furnish her own bedroom with whatever personal possessions would fit within those four walls. Plum, from the looks of the laden vehicles, was prepared to spill her belongings well beyond her allotted space. Dammit, Plum never did listen to directions.

Allison went forward in welcome, trying to rearrange her irritated countenance into a smile.

"Plum!"

"Oh, Allison, we're finally here. I declare, I didn't think we'd *ever* make it!" Plum's soft voice still carried a Tennessee accent, though she hadn't set foot in the south for forty years.

"Well, you're here now."

"I'm just exhausted. Such a trip!" She fanned herself ineffectually with a lace-bordered handkerchief. Plum was probably the last living soul in the country to carry real handkerchiefs. "Now the boys will just unload my things if you'll tell them where. Oh, Allison, it's just so *lovely* here!"

"Sit down and rest, Plum. You're to be in the south wing. I'll go and show the boys where to put your things."

The boys—men in their mid-forties—greeted Allison, refused coffee, expressed a desire to unload their mother's things and return immediately to Portland, all of which was agreeable to their hostess.

Two hours later they departed, having set up the big double bed, jockeyed the heavy dresser through the doorway, lugged the cedar chest and the rocker, hung the curtains that their mother had threaded onto rods, and carried box after overflowing box into the southeast bedroom until all the floor space was filled and cartons were stacked one atop another. After tearful farewells and maternal admonitions to drive carefully, they were gone.

"Oh, Allison, *tell* me I'm doing the right thing, coming here. I'm *so* afraid of making a mistake. What if it doesn't work out?"

"I can't tell you that you've done the right thing because I don't know yet. If it's not the right thing, we'll know it soon enough and we'll resolve it. Now, Plum, we've been all through this."

"Oh, but I *worry* so that it was dumb of me to sell my house."

"You were going to sell your house anyway and move to

an apartment. You just came here instead. I don't see any difference."

"I just worry so . . . "

"I know," said Allison and she did. "Look, if this doesn't work out, you just pack up your things and you go back to Portland and move into an apartment, as if Windom was just a little detour." Her brisk delivery suggested action, a whisking of hands one against the other, leaving behind one decision and moving promptly on to the next. That was Allison's way; it was not Plum's.

"I just *hope* I've done the right thing," she fretted.

Plum had arrived.

She had been born sixty-eight years ago, Victoria Belle Plumley, and the shortened surname had stuck probably because Victoria Belle was a name meant for a regal woman and Plum was short, dainty and rosy, dithery when anxious, serene when the anxiety fell away. She was a strong contrast to the tall and proud Allison. While kindly little Plum might be overlooked in a crowd, nobody ever overlooked Allison, with her dark hair exotically streaked with white at temples and forehead. While the cuddly Plum made adoring friends wherever she went, Allison glided through the world slip-covered with cool and distant dignity.

The two women had met more than thirty years ago when Allison, newly wed to her third husband, had moved next door to Plum, the wife of Judge Clovis Strawbridge. Clovis was gone now and Allison's third husband had long since been cast aside. It was the women's friendship which had endured.

Until she met Plum, Allison had never been interested in the friendship of women. Tiresome, boring creatures, she thought them. Inferior to men who did the interesting things in the world. Naturally Allison believed herself to be set apart from these other women. She was unafraid of power, she aspired to *do* rather than to watch others do, and so she scorned the company of women.

To be sure, Plum was very much a traditional woman—deferring to her husband, waiting, keeping herself in the background. Yet, in the very act of dismissing Plum as just another boring woman, Allison paused to take another look at her.

What she found was a luminous quality of acceptance which was rare in Allison's life. Plum simply accepted the eccentricity, the sharp tongue and opinionated declarations, the self-centeredness. Beguiled by such abundant good will, Allison had lowered her defenses long enough to make a friend. It had been a long and satisfying friendship.

And it was now to be tested.

Plum spent her first afternoon at Crooked House unpacking. Allison attempted to assist but Plum's methods were so haphazard, so without a sense of order, that Allison, appalled, had finally removed herself from the chaos and had gone for a long stroll on the beach. In the late afternoon she had prepared a delicate cream of asparagus soup for their supper, having put one of Beethoven's boisterous symphonies on the stereo to drown out Plum's clattery racket.

"My God, what have I done?" Allison muttered more than once.

After supper they sat together, exhausted for different reasons, and listened to the soothing lull of the Pacific.

"All right, Allison, tell me what the plan is. And don't say there's not a plan because I know you too well for that. You've planned *everything* down to the last teacup in the cupboard."

"Well, of course there's a plan." Allison fit a long cigarette into a filter holder which she used not for health's sake but because she enjoyed its dramatic effect. "I've told you what the plan is."

"Tell me again," insisted Plum, like a child who loves hearing a familiar story re-told.

Allison lit the cigarette, inhaled and propped her elbow on the sofa's velvety arm. "You and I will be here for two

weeks, settling in, getting used to one another and the way
we each do things—"

"Oh, Allison, we've been friends for thirty years. More.
Don't you think we know each other by now?"

"Being around one another is different from living under
the same roof." As a veteran of four marriages, Allison was
amply acquainted with this truth. "In two weeks, Jane will
come. That works out just fine. Jane needs time to finish up
some obligations in Portland. A poetry workshop she's
giving, or some such nonsense."

"Won't it be *won*derful! We'll be just like girls in the
dorm at college!"

Allison, who had never been to college, was annoyed.
"No, it will not be like that at all. We are not girls, Plum, we
are elderly women at the end of life, not starry-eyed know-
nothings just starting out."

"Oh." Plum was disappointed. "I thought we were going
to have fun. You make it sound so grim."

"Being old *is* grim."

Plum thought that over. "It's not *all* grim. Not for me,"
said this woman who had buried a husband and a son. "We
may not be young any more but I, for one, fully intend to live
out my life laughing when I can. *You* can do as you please."
She gave a feisty little nod to punctuate her declaration.

Allison inhaled again, watching as Plum serenely turned
yarn into colorful little squares, wondering as she had over
the years, what Plum actually did with all those squares; by
now she surely must have manufactured enough of the
damned things to blanket half the Cascade Mountain
Range. Allison was entirely ignorant of needlework and saw
no point in hobbies of any sort. When she was interested in
a subject—architecture, opera, photography, antiques—she
immersed herself into exhaustive research and experiential
study, then, satisfied, she turned to the next item of interest
on her life's agenda.

"Don't you mind being old?" Allison regarded her friend
with curiosity.

"No, I do not."

"Why not? And I warn you, I shall vomit if you recite idiotic drivel about basking in the golden sunset of life."

"Why should I mind being old? I've been young, and I've been middle-aged, and old is what's left to be. It's an orderly, natural progression, that's all." Plum studied the granny square she'd created with hook and yarn. "What I mind sometimes is the inconvenience of being old. It plain inconveniences me that I don't have all that energy I used to just take for granted. Or that I can't see a *thing* without my glasses. Or that my bones just don't move like they once did. That comes as a kind of surprise to me sometimes—I'll start to do something?—a simple thing, like going up unfamiliar stairsteps?—and I find myself moving so cautiously, as if I've quite *forgotten* how to manage. As I say, it's the inconvenience I object to."

"Well, yes," agreed Allison, squashing out her cigarette. "Growing old is inconvenient as hell."

"But you know what I find funny? It's that inside I feel just like *me*, like I'm the same essential person I always was. I guess I'd thought that might be different, that when I got to be old I'd feel wise and worldly and strong. But I don't. I still get puzzled over things, I'm still naive, I still get scared by life. Maybe the difference now is that I'm just more content with myself—I used to fuss at myself for being a scaredy-cat, and I don't do that any more because I know that there's just no *point* in fussing, no point at all." She said "a-tall" in the way of southern people, a habit which had grated on Allison's ears when they'd first met. Now it sounded so natural that Allison was rarely conscious of this and other remnants of Tennessee speech that colored Plum's conversations. It was one of those things that Allison had sought to alter in her friend (she could rarely resist trying to improve other people), but Plum had clung so contrarily to her dialect that Allison had finally admitted defeat.

"Do you feel that, Allison? Feel like you're still the same essential you inside?"

"Yes." Inside the seventy-two-year-old Allison there dwelt a four-year-old child who didn't know The Rules. Everyone else seemed to know them, seemed to have sprung from the womb with full knowledge of all The Rules which to Allison would remain always vague, mysterious, and indecipherable as she marched through life tripping over them, causing displeasure and consternation. There were some Rules, simple ones, that were carefully explained to her early on: "use this fork," "buy quality because it lasts," "take calculated risks with money," "art and music feed the soul." But there were other Rules that would forever be unknown to her, and she understood now that she, at seventy-two, was as distant from them as she'd been at four—how do you behave so that people will like you, love you, accept you? Allison had found ways to make people admire her, pay attention to her, marry her, even fear and envy her, but those other things, those foggy Rules, she still did not comprehend.

"Yes," she answered Plum, "inside I'm still the same me."

Plum smiled companionably at her friend and daintily snipped off the yarn from the completed square, tucking away the delicate small scissors, then flattening the colorful square with her dappled little hands.

"*There* now!" She stuffed her collection of crocheted handiwork into her yarn basket and stood up. "I'm going to bed now. I'm so tired I'm about to drop." She hesitated, unsure how to depart. "Well, this is the end of my first day here—"

"It will work out just fine, Plum. It will be just fine." And Allison hoped it would be.

Tommy Weed traveled light. He stuffed his clothes into the expensive gym bag that he'd ripped off from a health spa where he'd worked briefly and sat down on the dirty sleeping bag that covered the bed. He could still hear movement in the house which he shared with six other young people, and he intended to wait until it was quiet and then slip out unnoticed. He hadn't paid his share of the rent in two months. He smiled to himself, imagining the conversation that would take place when it finally dawned on those jerks that he was gone for good and that they were stuck with his bills. Served 'em right. Smart-ass creeps. In his pocket there were two tickets. One was for a bus ride that would take him out of Portland. The other was his ticket to freedom. This was the legacy from the father he'd never known, not until he'd traced the old man to a cancer ward in the prison hospital. Tommy didn't like sick people and he felt revulsion that this disgusting remnant of humanity, eaten away by disease, was his father. Still, the old man had finally, in the end, given his son something: a newspaper clipping carefully folded into a manila envelope and a laboriously written account of the part his father had played in a murder committed more than thirty years ago.

The house was quiet. Everybody had finally gone to bed.

Steathily he slipped out of the house.

Tommy Weed was on his way.

Chapter 2

JANE BROWNE had dressed herself off the racks at J.C. Penney's for more than forty years. She possessed virtually no sense of color coordination and had been known to appear in public wearing, among other jolting combinations, a flaming orange skirt with a magenta sweater. She was also sublimely unaware of textural compatibility, so that the ensembles she wore had an oddly embattled appearance. It was her naive habit to place herself at the mercy of sales clerks, some of whom were sensible, others no more discriminating than Jane herself, and all unable, in any case, to stand at her elbow as she rummaged through her closet and unerringly paired the most disagreeing colors.

There was, however, a curious social benefit from her generally unfortunate clothing selections: her appearance was unfailingly disarming. People rarely felt inferior or uneasy in Jane Browne's presence as they might well have, had she possessed more fashion sense. What Jane did possess was a keen and perceptive intelligence which she exhibited exuberantly, and while she often left her listeners amazed, she rarely left them alienated. She might be bright, they could console themselves, but just look at the God-awful way she dressed. Her most striking physical attributes were large fawn-like brown eyes and heavy chestnut hair which time had dulled but left almost entirely untouched by gray. She was a short woman, trim and compactly built, radiating an air of unflagging energy.

Jane Browne was a poet, not well known but rapturously appreciated by those who read her slim volumes of clear, sensitive verse. She had for many years subsidized her creative efforts by editing dull technical articles for a prosperous engineering firm. This tedious work had first given her discipline, then unleashed her longings to write soaring verse, which balanced those pedantic articles spawned by well paid, woefully unimaginative, and often nearly illiterate technocrats. When she decided to retire, move to Windom, and concentrate on writing poetry, her decision was not without trepidation, centered on an almost superstitious concern that her talent as a poet might vanish without its technical counterpart. Still, she was tired; it was time to leave all that tedious editing behind. And if her muse was inextricably linked to untangling technical stewpots, it would either find a new linkage or, regrettably, fade away, having given her succor when most it was needed.

These things occupied Jane's thoughts as she bounced along on the bus headed for the north coast. Two of her young admirers from the poetry workshop she'd just taught in Portland had offered to haul her spartan possessions to her new home. There was, alas, no room for a passenger in their battered truck so Jane had cheerfully boarded the bus, which now drew up at the Shell station at the edge of the village. Jane peered out the tinted bus window and laughed out loud as she spotted Allison and Plum seated with upright dignity in the Mercedes, as isolated as they could make themselves from the grimy tow trucks and overalled attendants at the service station. Jane rose, bumping up the aisle and down the steps with a canvas pack of books and a straw bag stuffed with overnight articles.

"My God!" Allison shuddered delicately as she beheld Jane.

"What?" Plum's brows furrowed in immediate concern.

"Never mind," muttered Allison. She sailed forward to greet Jane, who wore an unbecoming powder blue pants suit with a wholly unsuitable fire-engine red ruffled blouse. "You haven't changed a bit," she told Jane.

"Well, of course not, Allison—it's only been a few months

since you've seen me," Jane laughed. "Did the kids arrive all right with my things?"

"Oh, yes," said Plum happily, hugging Jane, ignoring powder blue and fire-engine red. "And we've got your room all fixed up for you. I mean, we didn't unpack your *personal* things but—why, even your bed's been made, just waiting for you!"

"Oh, what a loving thing for you to do. Did you get a chance to talk to the kids when they brought my stuff? They are such a dear couple from the poetry workshop. It was so thoughtful of them to offer to help me move."

"I'm surprised they made it in that awful truck," said Allison.

"But they did and isn't that wonderful?" Jane piled her belongings into the Mercedes. "Oh, how I loathe moving. Such a distressing business. I can hardly wait to see the house."

"It's just *lovely*. Allison has done such a *won*derful job remodeling it. You'll just love it, I know you will."

Plum patted Jane's arm affectionately, slipping easily into the well-worn role as peacemaker, mediator, untangler between her two friends. It was Allison's way to bicker and disagree with Jane, and this they all understood.

They settled themselves happily into the Mercedes and, with Allison at the wheel, glided majestically off toward Crooked House.

The young man with the yellow eyes watched them go, then wadded up his used bus ticket stub and tossed it carelessly onto the sidewalk. When things outgrew their usefulness to him, Tommy Weed got rid of them.

Allison introduced Jane to the view from her new bedroom window with the proprietary air of one whose personal responsibility it had been to assemble the scenery of crumbling old lighthouse and full expanse of wavy blue sea which surrounded it. Jane's delight in the spectacle was rewardingly spontaneous and complimentary; had it not been,

Allison was prepared to comment acidly on the sparseness of Jane's furnishings. How Jane could live like a medieval monk was beyond imagining. The bed was covered with an unadorned white spread, the lamps were functional, there were no pictures to be hung. Here in this room was economy of line, austerity, simplicity. Allison found these surroundings dismally depressing.

"I shall write many a verse in this room!" Jane's happy smile enveloped Allison, who promptly swallowed her comment that there certainly wouldn't be any distractions to sidetrack her efforts, and led the way to the dining room where Plum had set the table for luncheon.

"I wanted to make you something special for lunch, but it's hard when I don't really know very much about vegetarian cooking. I hope this will be all right. It's a kind of a rice souffle and here, these are mixed vegetables, all fresh. Mr. Brixby at the Gullway Market assured me of that."

Jane smiled warmly at Plum. "It smells superb."

"I never know what to do with people who eat only roots and berries." Allison's announcement was not new; she'd chastised Jane with it for years.

"Just roast the roots and boil the berries." Jane was unruffled.

"I never could imagine why on earth anyone would want to be a vegetarian."

"I myself don't care for pork," said Plum, "though I was reared on country ham. Is that souffle all right, Jane?"

"It's marvelously tasty."

"Needs salt," declared Allison.

"Actually, I became a vegetarian after my husband died," Jane said. "I had so little money then that I couldn't afford to buy meat. By the time I could afford it again, I'd lost a taste for it."

"I love a good steak," commented Allison.

Plum said quickly, "Maybe you could teach me how to make some vegetarian dishes, Jane. I don't think I'd like all those soybeans, though."

"I have an enticing recipe for a lasagne made with zucchini."

"I love a good steak."

Tommy Weed was carnivorous and, like most predators, skilled at living by his wits. He had disciplined himself to eat only one meal a day when necessary. He bought a box of crackers, a chunk of bologna, and a quart of milk at the Gullway Market for his evening meal. Although it would have been easy for him to pocket a block of cheese or a package of Twinkies, he did not allow himself this pleasure at the grocery store in Windom, not as a matter of ethics, but for practical reasons. He did not want to risk arrest on a petty shoplifting charge. Not when he was this close to big things.

He wasn't worried about finding a place to sleep, any more than about feeding himself. In a tourist town like Windom, it was easy enough to find a piece of plastic to spread on the sandy beach, sheltered by a big driftwood log. There was also a state park just south of the village, and he knew from experience that camping families were often hospitable and would share food or an old tarp with a quiet young man who looked hungry, especially if he presented himself as a sadly alienated, but salvageable youth. Tommy was a good actor.

He didn't need a job, not right away. He knew he could find work as a dishwasher or busboy during this busy tourist season. For now, what he needed most was time to study the situation, find a way to connect with the Crooked House inhabitants. He'd had no trouble finding the house and when he ambled past it, his first thought was that three old ladies would surely need help with the yard work. He didn't want to simply knock on their door, offering his services so obviously. No, this was too important to blow on some off chance that they might not need the grass cut.

Something would open that door to him. He was sure of that. And if not . . . ? His mouth twisted into a smile which framed his crooked teeth but did not reach his yellow eyes. If not? Well, what could three little old ladies do about it if he decided he wanted entry into their house?

In the first days of communal life, the women treated one another deferentially, chatting amiably about mutual acquaintances and interests, unearthing sweet memories of long-gone shared events.

By the sixth day, Allison had begun averting her eyes in annoyance whenever Plum embarked on another grandchild story. And it struck her as odd that she'd never before noticed how aggravatingly slow-moving Plum was; she seemed to dawdle endlessly over the simplest task. And most irritating was her goddamned agreeability to every suggestion Allison made.

Shall we have a bit of chicken for dinner?

Delightful!

Open the door to let in fresh air?

Please do!

Watch a movie on television?

A favorite!

But most of all was Plum's *thereness*. If Allison sat in the living room, Plum sat there too. If Allison walked on the beach, Plum's little footsteps were also imprinted in the sand. If Allison went to the village, Plum slid into the Mercedes's passenger seat right alongside. It was like having a round clingy shadow, and Allison's jaw ached from grinding her teeth in resentment.

While Allison's irritation focused on Plum, she found Jane's presence equally annoying. Her dietary preferences for wheat germ, tofu, yogurt, granola, and other repulsive-sounding edibles was a thrice daily reminder of their differences. And Jane had opinions on everything—oh, my God! did Jane have opinions. That Jane was articulate, well-read, and intelligent only exacerbated Allison's annoyance. There was no pleasing Allison. She was irritated when Jane held forth on some timely topic, when she secluded herself in her room to write, when she wafted about the house dreamily incommunicado, creating verses in her head. Allison couldn't decide which of these insufferably superior behaviors she disliked most.

Exactly one week after Jane's arrival, Allison went to her room and put on her long cardigan and broad-brimmed hat with the trailing feather.

"I'll be back in a while," she announced, her hand on the door knob.

"Where are you going?" Jane looked up from a pan of granola she was setting out to cool.

"Out."

"Where?" Plum's face lit up at the prospect of an excursion.

"Out! *Alone!*"

And Allison left, making her way cautiously down the stairs leading to the beach. It was the last weekend in June and the warm temperatures had coaxed tourists to the seaside. Allison walked slowly, not because of infirmity (her arthritic knee was genuinely painful at times, but far from disabling). She walked slowly because she felt angry and thwarted. It was not working out, this living with friends. If she found Plum and Jane exasperating after such a short time (and God knows, she certainly did) what would it be like a month from now with them all getting in each other's way, trespassing on nerves and feelings and space, telling and re-telling the same old stories? She must face the truth: she'd made a disastrous decision in bringing them all under one roof.

She was surprised to realize how far she'd walked when she saw the Seafarer condominium complex which was a good mile north of Crooked House. Allison paused to rest. She was too tired, too old to have to cope with such personality problems. Decisively, she made her way to the Seafarer restaurant.

Tommy Weed, who'd followed her from the house, watched Allison's progress toward the Seafarer. He sat down on a driftwood log to wait. The old lady just might have an accident on her way home and he wanted to be there when it happened.

The young man tending bar executed an authentic double-take as Allison swept into the lounge, the slender long feather on her hat trailing regally. She seated herself in a plushy chair and placed her heavily ringed hands expectantly atop the round table.

"Yes, ma'am?"

"Bring me a scotch on the rocks. A *double* scotch on the rocks."

"Double scotch rocks?" he goggled.

"Yes." She hissed the word unequivocally.

He went away to fix the drink, and Allison dug into her sweater pocket for her coin purse, extracted a five dollar bill, and wished she'd thought to bring her cigarettes and holder. She particularly liked to smoke when she felt angry or aggrieved. It gave her satisfaction to exhale smoke like an ill-tempered fire-breathing dragon.

The young man brought her drink and picked up the five dollar bill, then carefully counted out change.

"I don't suppose you smoke?"

"No, ma'am."

"It's a pity. For me. But perhaps just as well for you."

"There's a cigarette machine in the entryway."

"No, I don't like vending machines." She might have been referring to cobras. Allison was fond of well-executed personal service. She liked the power of rewarding those who performed well and withholding from those who did not.

The young bartender went away again but was back in a few minutes. On his tray, resting on a silly paper doily, was a filter-tipped cigarette. He extended the tray. "The cook smokes. This is regular, not menthol."

"You're a very nice young man. My thanks to the cook."

"Yes, ma'am."

She picked up a book of matches in the clean ashtray. They were emblazoned with *Seafarer* in scrolly script. She lit the cigarette, then sipped the drink thoughtfully. Beyond her, out the window, lay the silvery sea and the clean sweep of beach. Such magnificence, she thought, calming herself. Allison was a woman who deeply appreciated beauty.

She stayed an hour, watching the sea, watching the tourists cavorting on the beach, listening to the subdued noises the bartender made as he went about his work, listening without appreciation to the rock music that bleated from a small radio on the counter behind the bar. She and the young bartender were the only two people in the place, it being still too early on a weekday afternoon for other patrons.

"Now, we aren't getting on each other's nerves," she mused, glancing at the bartender. "He goes about his business, wiping and polishing; I go about mine, drinking and sea-gazing. Why can't it be like this for Plum and Jane and me? Oh, well, if I sat here long enough, that would probably change too. Things have a way of changing. He'd start telling me boring stories about cars or whatever young men talk about these days, and I'd probably start telling him how to do his job more efficiently, meddling the way I generally do . . . ."

She left him a generous tip nonetheless.

Allison, who rarely drank doubles of anything, particularly hard liquor, was feeling tiddly as she made her way uncertainly back down to the beach. Well, no matter if she were a wee bit tiddly, she reassured herself, she *did* feel better.

So self-absorbed was she, Allison did not notice the skinny young man who sprawled leisurely on the driftwood log. She also failed to notice his darting foot, but was aware only of tripping. "That damned double scotch," she thought dizzily as she pitched forward.

Tommy rose and walked toward her.

"What do you mean, it's broken?" Allison sat in regal disarray on a driftwood log on the beach, demanding an answer of the hapless paramedic who squatted before her.

"I don't know how else to say it, ma'am. Your wrist is probably broken." He had added the "probably" in the face of her irascibility.

"Are you a doctor?"

"No, ma'am, I'm an emergency medical technician. That's why I'm here. I'm assigned to the Windom Beach Patrol. Somebody called in about an accident on the beach and I was dispatched to investigate. That's my job."

"Well, my wrist can't be broken."

"Yes, ma'am." The paramedic was agreeing that he'd heard her statement, not that he concurred in her diagnosis. He marveled at the way this old lady could sit on the sandy driftwood log, hat askew, skirt hiked up, and still manage to maintain an indisputable air of authority. According to witnesses she'd tripped and fallen, landing on her right wrist.

"Well, ma'am, as you say, I'm not a doctor. I think a doctor should have a look at it though. If you like, I'll drive you to Dr. Woodring's office in the village."

"I will not be carted around in that ambulance like an invalid. It's a simple bruised wrist." It was sufficient mortification that she be the center of all this unwanted attention, the gaping tourists, their tittering offspring, and their yapping dogs, all looking at her as if she were a doddery old fool. She glanced up into the indecisive face of the paramedic. "But thank you for your assistance. You've done your job, and done it well. So now you can go. I'll just sit here a moment to rest, then be on my way."

"Well, now, ma'am—I don't believe I can just leave you here like this."

"I'll be fine. I live just right up there at Crooked House."

The paramedic looked at her helplessly with visions of the old lady passing out, having a heart attack, God knows what, and him being held responsible for not insisting she go to the doctor regardless of her preferences.

"How about if I walk you up to your house?" asked a young man in the crowd of gawkers. He spoke quietly and

Allison, eager for this humiliating scene to be done with, agreed immediately.

"Okay," said the paramedic with considerable relief, then added an aside to the rescuer, "Try to get her to the doctor, will you?"

Allison allowed Tommy Weed to hold her arm as they made their way across the beach and up the wooden stairs to Crooked House.

"Now you take your time on these steps," Tommy cautioned. "They're pretty steep."

"Yes, yes, I know. I intend to have new ones installed before someone gets injured."

By the time they reached the house, Tommy had convinced Allison to allow him to drive her to the doctor who, half an hour later, had examined the wrist, concurring in the patient's own diagnosis of a severe sprain, not a broken bone. Tommy drove her home again, Plum and Jane perched in the back seat of the Mercedes, excitedly recounting the fright they'd sustained when they'd realized the ambulance had been called down on the beach to Allison's rescue. And they agreed that the paramedic and now this young man had indeed been most considerate.

When he deposited the women back home, Tommy refused the ten dollar bill Allison tried to press on him.

"Oh, no, I'm just glad I was there to help."

"Please. I insist."

But Tommy was firm. "No, Mrs. Moffitt. It wouldn't be right for me to take your money." Not a measly ten dollars, he thought. I've got much bigger bucks in mind. I've got you where I want you because now, old lady, you owe me something.

Allison did not sleep well that night. She kept waking up, at first with a vague sense of disquiet which, several hours before dawn, crystallized into a definite fear. Somehow, in all her meticulous planning, she had overlooked the dismaying fact that neither Plum nor Jane drove an automobile. Plum was far too nervous to drive any more, having mowed down a parking meter one disastrous day when she mistook the accelerator for the brake pedal. Jane hadn't had a license in years, having gotten around Portland by public transportation, taxis, and rides solicited from accomodating friends.

Damn! If only they were all younger. Jane could re-learn to drive, and Plum could get over that silliness about being nervous behind the wheel. No, maybe not that. It was probably in the best interests of village pedestrians that Plum maintain her position as passenger. Could they simply walk the mile to the village for groceries and mail? Or maybe Jane could ride her bicycle to do their necessary errands. This was the whole problem with growing old, one's alternatives diminished. Still, Allison had not lived all these years without honing her problem-solving skills to a fine point. Satisfied that every problem had a solution, even if it weren't immediately apparent, Allison finally slept.

The solution presented itself at eleven o'clock the following morning with the appearance of Tommy Weed at the door.

"I just wondered how you were feeling today, Mrs. Moffitt."

"I'm fine. It's a bother not to be able to use my hand but I'm fine. It's thoughtful of you to ask." Allison's tone was dismissive, but Tommy lingered.

"Well, actually, I was wondering if you needed any errands run or anything. See, I couldn't take any money yesterday for doing something that was just the right thing to do—" Miraculously, the words did not stick in his throat. "But—well, here's the thing, I've been looking for work and I'm real handy with tools or in the yard. Or if, maybe you need a driver, or just somebody to run errands for you till your wrist heals—"

Allison hesitated. In the shock of her fall yesterday, she had paid scant attention to Tommy Weed. He'd been merely a useful way out of an embarrassing situation. Now as she looked at him more carefully, standing on her doorstep in the bright morning sunlight, she felt a pang of uncertainty.

He was a most unprepossessing young man, with those awful crooked teeth, those strange yellowish eyes. Still, no one was more expert than Allison on the deceptiveness of appearances—and he had been very kind yesterday. Lord knows, it would be inconvenient not to have transportation to the village for mail and food. Within a week, surely the pain in her wrist would have diminished so that she could drive again.

After all, what harm could come of hiring Tommy Weed for a week?

Chapter 3

THE VILLAGE of Windom had not allowed Coast Highway 101 to scissor through its heart, but had instead nestled itself into the hills and trees a safe distance from that racing thoroughfare. In its early years of lazy development this arrangement had been ideal for the wealthy folks who built imposing beach houses along the pristine Pacific shoreline. In time, however, as the general population exploded in reproduction, as transportation improvements made the oceanside more accessible to greater numbers of travelers, and as real estate developers saw big money in coastal properties, Windom reluctantly joined the commercial parade.

The business section, a grandiose misnomer, consisted of three short blocks lying perpendicular to the ocean and a good six blocks from it. The humble collection of utilitarian shops had been seen by the cold eyes of developers as irredeemably shabby, but not without potential. One early group of cost-efficiency experts had favored razing the whole three blocks and replacing them with the instant tried-and-true: the Colonel and his chicken, McDonald's golden arches, Dairy Queen soft ice cream, and a Safeway grocery. Happily, more thoughtful heads had prevailed, insisting that there was no need to destroy this village in order to save it. What the business area required was a face-lift, went this theory, not radical surgery.

And so Orin Brixby's tiny general store had expanded into the Gullway Market where the prices were higher than at a chain grocery, but the produce was fresh and the service, though unhurried, was friendly. And Fudgie Pike's candy store got bright pink-and-white striped awnings and new paint, and sold the same delightful salt water taffy and wickedly caloric chocolate concoctions as before. Mr. Jarvis at the bank, who still wasn't convinced that going off the gold standard had been such a hot idea, grudgingly erected a new building that beckoned customers inside with hanging plants and framed watercolors by local artists. Con Snyder persuaded some investors to build Sea Sprite Square, a mini-mall of specialty shops offering beachwear, books, candles, kites, and curiosities fashioned from agates, shells, and driftwood.

There were those who felt that the Blue Dolphin Tavern should re-locate, preferably in Seattle, but more tolerant voices held that folks who liked to relax by drinking beer, playing darts or video games, and joining in sing-alongs had a right to a place to entertain themselves, too. So Dolph stayed in his old location next to the Shell station and spruced up the outside of his tavern as a gesture to progress. Inside, the Blue Dolphin steadfastly remained the same— dark, beery, inviting.

Enter the beautifiers, those unsung souls who understand, more than any mere MBA ever could hope to, that a business community does not thrive by peddling trinkets and staples alone. The diligent advocates of beauty, many of the same people who were the energetic force behind building a library and renovating an old church into an Arts Center, insisted on brick walkways around the shops, benches for the weary to sit upon, flower boxes bursting forth with petunias, begonias, verbena and flowering kale. With determined enthusiasm, they hung pots of posies from the lamp posts and planted shrubs in community parking lots. The village of Windom emerged from all this with an endearing (some said suffocating) quaintness.

This was Windom, however, not Eden. The developers, seeing what good the ambience of quaint had wrought, believed that the sky was now the limit. While the brick-layers and basket-hangers were busily beautifying the heart of the village, the bulldozers were hard at work on a stretch of beachfront property northwest of the downtown area.

Con Snyder, who was a mighty believer in God, country, and dollar bills, though not necessarily in that order, dreamed of turning Windom into a bustling resort community, beginning with his Seafarer Condominium complex. Windom had but four motels, and these were family-owned and purposely unobtrusive. Three of them squatted beside Highway 101 to entice auto traffic; the fourth was tucked away modestly a few blocks off the center of town.

One reason for the paucity of motels was that virtually no beachfront property was available for building. The early settlers of Windom had been wealthy people who had built their large, often two-storied, vacation homes in a row along the beach. The street which ran along these homes, though officially named Ocean Drive, was referred to by the locals as Rich Row. As the streets descended from the beach toward the town, the houses became increasingly modest. On the south flank of Rich Row there was a heavily wooded area, now a state park. To the north of Rich Row was a single block of simple beachfront houses where dwelled some year-round families who had long ago had the good sense or the dumb luck to build on what was to become prime property. Severing this block of little houses was a beach access road and to the north of that was the grandly sprawling Seafarer condo complex.

The battle lines were cleanly drawn between Con Snyder's damn-the-environment-full-speed-ahead growth forces and the stubbornly cautious preservationists. The war, now in its eighth year, was expected to last for decades.

Like residents in resort communities the world over, the locals of Windom had an ambivalent attitude toward the tourists who were the backbone of their economy. The locals would have been just as pleased if the tourists had stayed at home and maintained a mail-order relationship ("Enclosed is your order of a packet of sand, a tin of sea air, a tape of seagull cries. Kindly remit check or money order . . .").

But business, alas, depended upon the physical presence of these cash-laden itinerants, their comfort catered to and their ever-increasing numbers tolerated. So while the residents, of necessity, welcomed the tourists, the truth was that most villagers did not really want these outsiders cluttering up the lovely beaches with their trash, their loud music, their obstreperous drunkenness and often, sadly, their ignorance of or cruelty to the sea life they'd come to behold. (Why, for instance, would a human being shoot an arrow through the heart of a sea bird? *Why?*) The admonition that visitors should take only photographs and memories and leave only footprints on the sand was, too often, ignored.

The villagers of Windom knew all about Allison Moffitt's sprained wrist. They knew she'd summarily sent the paramedic on his way, knew she'd visited Dr. Woodring's office, knew the diagnosis and the prognosis.

On the Friday morning after the accident they got the next installment. Tommy Weed chauffered the old ladies into the village in the Mercedes, gallantly leaping out to open doors, then standing guard while the elderly trio tottered off to tend to their shopping.

At the Citizen's Village Bank, Nedry Jarvis unfolded himself and sent a tiny glacial smile in Mrs. Moffitt's general direction. He avoided direct eye contact whenever possible, but Mrs. Moffitt was, after all, a wealthy customer and so received a smile and a glance, both fleeting. Mr. Jarvis treated most of his clientele as if they were direct descendants of Bonnie and Clyde.

"So sorry to hear of your injury," he intoned mournfully.

Allison, who was accustomed to being treated respectfully by bankers, was surprised that news of her indisposition had preceded her into the village. A lifelong city person, she expected general anonymity. She'd already been warned by Mr. Rainwater at the post office to take care when strolling on the beach, and even the clerk in the stationer's shop had made solicitous inquiries about her injury. Allison didn't know it, but Plum and Jane were also collecting expressions of sympathy on her behalf.

Orin Brixby at the Gullway Market informed Plum that he'd first understood that Mrs. Moffitt had broken her hip and was very much relieved to know the actual injury was far less severe. A few minutes later, Fudgie Pike at the candy store next door regaled Plum with a lengthy account of how she herself had once sustained not one but *two* broken arms from a tumble down the stairs, so it clearly paid to be cautious.

Meanwhile, at the Village Pharmacy, Jane was the proxy recipient of a lecture on osteoporosis and the wisdom of the ingestion of daily calcium tablets by females in midlife. This lecture was delivered by Mr. Stooper, the pharmacist, a man left so shrunken and brittle by time that he looked as if he might profit by swallowing some of his own elixirs.

The women met at the Tea Cozy after their round of shopping. "I declare," said Plum, "everywhere I went people were asking about your sprained wrist, Allison. News certainly travels fast in this village."

"You'd think they'd have more interesting things to discuss." Allison's tone was tart, partly because she was still chagrined over the accident and partly because the friendly curiosity of the villagers was so unexpected. She was also grateful that the young paramedic had apparently kept his mouth shut about her tiddly state at the time of the accident. The less said about *that* the better. If such an uninteresting tidbit as a sprained wrist enraptured the villagers, they would have a veritable feast with her slight and wholly uncharacteristic inebriation.

Orin Brixby watched Allison and her friends emerge from the Tea Cozy and walk toward their car. He'd observed Tommy Weed lounging proprietarily against the Mercedes while the women had gone about their errands.

"Who is that fellow?" he asked his wife, Winnie Ruth.

She didn't even have to look up from rearranging cabbages

in the bins to know who her husband meant. "I don't know.
I've been keeping an eye on him though."

This did not surprise Orin. Winnie Ruth kept an eye on
everybody. She was as distrustful as Nedry Jarvis over at the
bank, and with much better reason. Winnie Ruth's watchful
glint had deterred more shoplifters at the Gullway Market
than the tacked-up posters threatening prosecution of the
light-fingered.

"He's been in here, skulking around. But he's paid for
everything." She made this last comment grudgingly. Winnie Ruth liked apprehending shoplifters. She'd yell loudly at
them, order them to put their pilferings back on the shelf,
and send them out of the store in a verbal shower of disgrace.
Occasionally, if she were especially vexed with the attitude of
a miscreant, she would summon Police Chief Kirksey to the
scene. Winnie Ruth tolerated no nonsense.

"Well, look at him, would you—opening doors for the
ladies, putting away their packages." Orin peered around a
cookie display, craning his neck toward the window. "You
gotta admit, he's sure polite and helpful."

It was Winnie Ruth's opinion that nobody under fifty
exhibited good manners any more, and she stood ready to
revise that age limit upward at the height of the tourist
season. Tommy Weed's show of manners did not impress
her.

When the ladies were comfortably tucked into the car,
Tommy asked them if they'd like to take a little spin down
the coast, and they agreed that this was a fine idea. Although
Jane coolly regarded Tommy as untrustworthy, she was
relieved to have a confident young driver at the wheel; in her
view, Allison's driving habits were alarmingly erratic. The
June day was warm, the Pacific shimmered in the sunshine.
When they returned home, Tommy nosed the car skillfully
into the garage, locked it, and handed the keys to Allison
with a little bow. He carried their packages into the house,
then departed, whistling a cheerful little tune.

The ladies agreed he was a very helpful young man.

Sunday was a day which stretched long for a single person like Tommy Weed, even in a lively resort community. He'd risen early that morning from the sleeping bag he'd swiped from a camper at the state park where he was staying. He'd managed to make himself comfortable there, stealing and scavenging whatever he needed from his transient neighbors. He'd stashed his things in some bushes (can't be too careful of thieves) and had walked into the village where he found a little restaurant that offered a hearty breakfast for a few dollars. He'd ambled, bored, around the streets for a while until he noticed the nice fat Sunday paper in the dispenser by the Blue Dolphin Tavern. He hung around until a motherly-looking lady came along who seemed inclined to believe his story that he'd been cheated out of his newspaper by the dispenser and had no more change. She allowed Tommy to help himself to a paper when she opened the box for her own. Tommy thanked her, then smirked at her departing back. Why pay for something you can get free by using your brains? He took the paper to a sunny bench and skimmed through it, then stuffed it into a trash barrel so nobody else could have it. He again took to the street. It had turned warm so he stopped into the Gullway to buy a can of pop, ostentatiously paying for it, recognizing the distrust in Winnie Ruth's eyes which he'd seen in many storekeepers over the years. He smiled politely but she merely stared at him. He called her a stupid bitch in his mind and went out the door, insolently letting it bang behind him.

He looked down, then up the street. That seemed to be all there was to this hick place. Tommy liked cities, liked the anonymity of crowded sidewalks. Hell, he even liked the traffic noises. There were places to hide in the city. Here, he felt exposed. He sat down on the porch steps in front of the market, lit a cigarette, and winking the smoke away from his eyes, flipped open the lid of the Coke can.

There were cedar benches along the walls of the market and the candy store next to it. Sprawled on these benches were three teenaged boys, all knees and elbows and unreliable voices, poking and hitting each other, making jokes, laughing. Tommy regarded them judgmentally. Jerks. Tommy was a loner, had never had boyhood friends. When he was a child and saw other boys his own age cavorting like these kids, he'd assumed they were making fun of him, which only occasionally was true. He distrusted them, never sought their company, didn't need them, would never act stupid like they did. He gave the boys a disdainful glance and turned his attention to the parade of tourists meandering along the sidewalks. He had a good eye for people who would be easy targets, although Tommy was not a pickpocket. Oh, occasionally he might help himself to something that was just begging to be swiped. He might take a wallet from a woman's handbag if she'd left it carelessly on a counter or in a shopping cart or swinging open by a strap from her shoulder. People like that needed to be taught a lesson, in Tommy's opinion. They got what they deserved for being so careless.

Yeah, he knew how to pick out victims. Stay away from women who looked like screamers or hitters. Go for the ones who looked like scared rabbits, the ones who looked like they might be too embarrassed to make a fuss. They usually were, and it made him laugh; they'd rather be robbed than make a scene. He glanced up at a young woman who was walking toward him. Now, her, he'd be wary of. That one would fight back, she wouldn't be scared to make a scene, she'd yell her bloody head off. He watched her approach. She was about the age of the teenage boys sitting on the bench. They had noticed her too, and were poking each other, guffawing in juvenile delight as she came closer. One of the boys whispered a dare to another who half rose and blurted out, "Hey, baby, where you going?"

The young woman looked at him levelly, then said, "Get lost." Her voice was at once firm and tolerant.

The boy turned red and sank back down on the bench in a shower of derisive hoots from his friends.

Suddenly the door of the market swung open and its owner stood there, wiping his hands on his white apron.

"Carolina?"

"Afternoon, Mr. Brixby."

"Everything okay?"

"Oh, yes."

A look passed between them which Tommy caught and interpreted accurately: in this village, we look after our own. We belong here and you do not, so watch your step. Carolina continued on her way down the street and unobtrusively, Tommy's gaze followed her. He might steal from passive women who begged to be victimized, but it was females like this Carolina who caused a thrilling ripple in his stomach. It was not passion but a yearning to dominate, to see a strong woman beg for mercy. His mercy. All those years his mother had been the strong one, but in time, even she had pleaded with him for mercy. Finally, she had feared him. And with good reason. Tommy had a good memory for wrongs done him. She paid the price, and so had that other one, that social worker busybody with all her education and her superior ways. He'd shown her a thing or two about dominance. She, too, had finally feared him. Oh, yes, the mighty toppled and were overcome with fear, begging for mercy. Fear and mercy. Fear and mercy. The words roared in his head like the pounding ocean. Fear and mercy . . . .

Chapter 4

SUNDAY WAS A day which Mr. Bertram, Windom's leading contractor, did not mind spending alone and so had declined his wife's invitation to visit her sister's family, but chose instead to leisurely read the Sunday paper, then doze blissfully off to the serenade of a wildlife special on television. When the ringing phone woke him suddenly he had to ponder for a moment where he was—stalking a wildebeest in the wilds of Africa or wandering in the political jungle of *Doonesbury*. He stretched out his hand unenthusiastically and picked up the telephone.

"Hallo?"

"Mr. Bertram?"

"Speaking."

"This is Allison Moffitt."

"Why, hello, Mrs. Moffitt. How're you?"

"Very well, thank you."

"Everything all right at Crooked House?"

"That's why I'm calling, Mr. Bertram."

"What's the problem?" Bert's defenses geared up for action.

"There's no problem at all. I recalled that you expressed an interest in seeing the house when it was furnished, and I'm calling to invite you to come this afternoon, if it's convenient."

Bert was surprised. He'd imagined she would let this invitation lapse once she'd moved into the house. "Why, that would be fine," he told her.

"I'll expect you at three then," she said and hung up.

Bert was a craftsman more comfortable with sweet-smelling cedar than with people. He had his own methods of working and did not take well to interference, holding tenaciously to the view that skill, expertise, and dedication to purpose were far more valuable than public relations. Besides, wood was predictable, whereas people were not. You cut a board in two and it stayed cut. People, now, they were forever reassembling themselves, changing their minds, having second thoughts, creating new ideas and new problems. Nope, give him wood over people any day.

Bert became particularly aware of his preference for wood over people not long after he'd been hired to do the remodeling on Crooked House. Uncharacteristically, he took to dropping into the Blue Dolphin Tavern after his day's work. Rarely reticent among his peers, he soon let it be known that he was experiencing great exasperation at the hands of one Allison Nichols Ashmore Wyatt Moffitt. He reeled off this string of names triumphantly, as if the many marriages of Mrs. Moffitt were indisputable testimony to her capacity to cause a man grief.

"What does she do that gets you so riled up?" asked Dolph, the owner of the tavern and a leading dispenser of village gossip.

"Do? What she does is she sits herself on a bench right out there on the lawn and she watches me work, that's what she does!"

"Well, now, Bert—"

"I'm not finished. She sits there watching me and when she wants my attention she whacks her damned cane on the bench. 'Mr. Bertram! Mr. Bertram!' " His voice rose to falsetto and his mouth twisted itself into a prissy shape. " 'What are you doing there, Mr. Bertram?' She wants to know a reason for *everything*. That old lady is driving me crazy." He shook his head and morosely took in a slow stream of beer.

"Do you answer her when she asks what you're doing?" Dolph imagined, erroneously, that he'd tell that old lady in no uncertain terms what she might like to do with that cane of hers.

Bert sighed heavily. "Of course, I answer her. It's her house and it's her money. At first, I didn't mind." And indeed he had not. Bert took pride in his work and was not averse to giving meandering explanations to those who were interested. And he had to admit that Allison Moffitt was certainly interested. "I guess I even encouraged her some at first," he admitted, for he was a fair man. "Hell, she seemed like a nice old lady. Sharp as a tack, too." He did not elaborate on the surprises he'd sustained at her quick perceptive comments, her keen questions.

"She a retired businesswoman?"

"Don't know. She could be a retired madam. Or gun-runner, for all I know. She's one smart old lady."

As the work progressed on Crooked House, however, Bert had cut back on his talebearing, a little ashamed of himself for complaining to his cronies about an old lady who wasn't there to defend herself. Any stranger to Windom made an easy target for ridicule by the villagers who, by long habit, banded securely together to discuss the merits and defects (particularly the latter) of any candidate for inclusion in their closed society. Although Bert could not have articulated this classic group behavior dynamic, he did recognize the discomfort he felt at his one-sided reportage.

"So how are things going with that old lady up at Crooked House?" asked Dolph one evening. He felt it was his civic duty to keep abreast of village events, being that the local newspaper came out only weekly and then only to officially chronicle items that everybody already knew anyway.

Bert watched the familiar motion of the barman wiping the counter, fascinated as always by the sight of the tattooed serpent writhing from the hairy underbrush of Dolph's forearm as if in pursuit of the damp rag. Dolph grinned invitingly, anticipating entertainment.

Bert didn't deliver it. "Oh, well—you know, she's really not so bad. She just wants to be sure things are done the way she wants 'em done. Can't say that I really blame her for that."

Disappointed, Dolph tried another strategy. "Does she know about that curse on Crooked House?" He was not above creating instant folklore to dangle before gullible patrons in the tavern.

Bert sighed. It was his opinion that Dolph would haul his own grandmother onto the auction block for three dollars. "Crooked House doesn't have a curse on it, and don't you go telling that around."

Unabashed by this admonition Dolph, always the gleaner of information, persisted, "When are those old ladies gonna be moving in?"

"Don't know and didn't ask."

Now that it was all over, Bert liked to believe that he'd always been warmly tolerant of Mrs. Moffitt's insistence on presiding over his work. His memory had melted all their interactions into a kind of camaraderie, and the sound of her whacking cane and her imperious voice had smoothed out into points of benevolent amusement.

He did, however, clearly recollect their most intense moment of dissension. He'd been working away, humming tunelessly to himself, crunching curls of shavings beneath his heavy boots, and had heard the unmistakable purr of her Mercedes as it glided majestically into the driveway. He'd watched her emerge from the car wearing full rain regalia—boots, dark stockings, a belted raincoat, a broad-brimmed rainhat—and carrying an umbrella which she pressed into multiple service as cane and pointer as well as rain-shedder. She greeted him civilly but without particular warmth, then commenced her inspection tour. Courtesy or pride or eagerness to please, perhaps all of these, compelled Bert to accompany her, padding bearlike behind her elegantly upright back.

"This window," she observed, pointing peremptorily with her spike-tipped umbrella, "I distinctly ordered a fixed window for this room. This one has a sliding panel which opens, Mr. Bertram."

"Well, ma'am, it does because code says you have to have an egress from a bedroom."

"An egress?"

"An opening," Bert clarified unhappily. "So you can get out—in case of fire, for instance."

"If I can get out, then someone can get in, isn't that true?"

"I'd say so. . . ."

"I want a fixed window here, Mr. Bertram, a window that cannot be opened from the outside by an intruder."

"Well now, ma'am, I can't go against code. And code says you gotta have an egress in a bedroom." Bert's voice had taken on a distinctly stubborn tone.

"Hmmph." Her posture, as she moved away from him, suggested that she did not care for lectures on building codes from the hired help.

Later, Bert saw her with a tape measure at the window carefully peering through her trifocals at the numbers which she jotted down in a black leather notebook. He had not the least doubt that he hadn't heard the last about fixed bedroom windows, and indeed he had not. Mrs. Moffitt made a spectacular visit to the building inspector in an attempt to get her own way, but had failed. Bert was puzzled that the old lady had given in so meekly, but was relieved that she apparently held no animosity over his insistence upon following the code. Actually, he admired her tenacity, her decisiveness, and her shrewd attention to detail. Bert, an honest and conscientious man, could tolerate her scrutiny of his work.

He hadn't seen Mrs. Moffitt since the completion of the remodeling of Crooked House. When the job was done, he had followed her through the house and said, when the inspection was finished, that he'd sure like to see the place when it was all fixed up.

"Would you now?" she'd asked, running her hand over a door frame in the kitchen.

"Yes, ma'am, I sure would. She sure looks different now than when we started."

"That was the whole point, Mr. Bertram." She whipped out the leather note-book from her purse and wrote down his name, and he felt foolishly pleased to be included in that mysterious little book of hers.

At three o'clock on Sunday afternoon Bert strolled up to the front door of Crooked House, casting a professional eye over his own handiwork, feeling pride in it. Yes sir, he'd done a good job here.

Despite the sinister reputation which the proprietor of the local tavern tried to create for it, Crooked House delighted Bert. It had begun life as an unremarkable cottage built in the years just before the Depression. At the end of World War II it had been sold to a family with several children, and the north wing had been constructed, angled to capture the magnificent ocean view. In the fifties it had been sold to another family, this one with many children, and they'd added the south wing, hoping to achieve balance. Ten years later, new owners had enlarged the central living area, giving Crooked House the look of a turtle, neck out-stretched, lurching seaward. It was this collection of sprawled wings and juttings that Allison Moffitt had purchased.

Bert approved of her decision not to add on to Crooked House; indeed, she could not have done so had she desired, for there was no room for expansion save upward. Nope, in his opinion, Mrs. Moffitt wisely sought to solidify, to make comfortable and attractive what was already there. With his competence backed by a great deal of her money, she had laid siege to Crooked House, ripping out walls and windows and doors, then carefully building into this shell her own impressive style.

"And on the seventh day she rested," murmured Bert, as he reached out to ring the bell. The door opened promptly and there stood the mistress of Crooked House.

Bert knew nothing of women's fashions, but he readily recognized the excellence of Mrs. Moffitt's ensemble. As she had not stinted on the cost of materials for her house, neither, he guessed, did she stint on the cost of her wardrobe. He could not identify silk or cashmere, but he was certain that her whole get-up cost more than his wife spent on clothes in a year. Gold glistened at Mrs. Moffitt's ears, and on her fingers were the diamond trophies of her four marriages.

"Come in, Mr. Bertram."

Bert entered, uneasily aware that tromping around raw board floors in this house, stepping over his tools and around sawhorses, he had been in his natural element. Here, now, with carpeting and drapes and polished furniture, he became acutely aware of his bulk, of his heavy boots, of the denim work clothes that were his uniform. He stuffed his hands into his pockets. His arms felt long, his hands hammy.

Mrs. Moffitt introduced him to the two women who sat like well-behaved youngsters in the parlor. Bert ducked his head in their direction and, now feeling bashful as well as elephantine, mumbled greetings and wished he were back in his own home reading the Sunday comics.

Allison led him through the house, commenting briefly on how pleased she was with this or that idea, which had been the subject of many debates during construction. He was a little surprised when she led him to the north wing to view the bedrooms, having had some idea that she might regard these as too private to be displayed. But no, she flung open the door to her own room, and Bert gaped. Here was a nest of luxury, the likes of which he'd never seen except in a movie. There was an ornately carved antique bed, a matching dresser with a marble top, pale silken draperies, a brocade chaise, exquisite lamps and figurines. Bert wished he'd brought his wife to view this opulence. No, perhaps not; it would just create dissatisfaction. He'd best left Emily visiting at her sister's.

The southeast room belonged to the lady introduced to

him as Plum. It was a riotously fussy room with immaculate ruffled curtains swathing the windows, afghans, cushions, flowers, photographs, lusty green plants, frilly shaded lamps, sun-catchers, watercolor paintings, ruffles, laces, flounces, scalloped edges. It was a feast of pastels and soft shapes, rather than just clutter, and while it gave Bert a momentary sense of disorientation, he recognized something compellingly sweet about this room, like an old-fashioned valentine.

By the time he'd viewed Jane's spartan room, he'd begun to relax a little.

"Well?" Allison's voice was amused. "What do you think?"

"It's all so—unusual," said Bert, struggling to find an apt description.

"Yes, it is." Allison gave him a wry smile.

Bert's gaze fell on the windows, and it was his turn to deliver a wry smile. "I see you got around the code to get the windows you wanted."

Mrs. Moffitt came close to smirking. "Oh, yes." She had simply ordered virtually impenetrable storm windows installed over all the windows.

"Well, don't go playing with any matches then. You sure can't get out of those windows in a hurry."

"And nobody can get in them either." Mrs. Moffitt led him back to the living room where Plum had laid out lavish refreshments.

"A goddamned tea party!" thought Bert, and worried that his table manners might not withstand the scrutiny of this feminine company. Bert liked situations where he knew the expected behavior. In the Blue Dolphin he never even thought of manners. The Blue Dolphin—God, if they could see him now, tea-partying with a gaggle of old ladies!

But the chair offered him was comfortable, the coffee strong, the cake light, and before long Bert was enjoying himself immensely, recalling for the ladies how the village had changed over the years. He was astounded when finally he glanced at the old clock on the mantel to realize that he'd been there for two hours.

At the door, Allison mentioned that she'd hired Tommy Weed to drive for her and do odd jobs around the place.

Bert frowned. "He's not local. What does he look like?"

Allison described Tommy Weed.

"Yeah, I've seen him around." In the Blue Dolphin, to be precise. A disappointed-looking kid who didn't get much pleasure out of life and, from the looks of him, didn't give much either.

"He said he came to Windom looking for summer work," explained Allison. "We used to call them drifters, you know. Now it's more socially accepted for young people to wander about the country—finding themselves, they call it."

Bert had never had to find himself; he'd never been lost. He'd always known who he was: a plain man with a talent for working with his hands, an ordinary villager who'd never seen anything much of the outside world but knew instinctively that he was unlikely to find anything better than what he had right here in Windom where his roots ran deep.

"Well, I'd warn you to take care. Strangers—" He shook his head, leaving his dark opinion of strangers unspoken.

"Oh, I'm sure he's harmless. I'm a very good judge of people, Mr. Bertram."

"Hmmm." Bert was a good judge of people also. And there was something about Tommy Weed that made him uneasy.

Plum set out a bowl of milk for the black half-grown cat that had been hanging around the back door for the past week. Allison did not approve of keeping pets, but Plum could not endure the sight of a hungry creature. Disgraceful the way people discarded animals on the beach. No sense of responsibility. Plum intended to feed the cat, encouraging it to make itself at home. In time, when Allison got accustomed to the idea of seeing it around, Plum would invite it inside; by Christmas that cat would be curled in front of the fireplace snoozing happily. Plum hadn't reared four boys without learning a trick or two.

She straightened, watched for a moment as the cat eagerly lapped up the milk, then turned her attention to Tommy who was polishing the Mercedes. He certainly liked sprucing up that car. Washing, waxing, cleaning, carefully giving it a high shine. Plum admired that because she, too, enjoyed the satisfying labor of cleaning.

She also liked to cook, and was pleased to have people to cook for. Jane was woefully deficient in culinary practices, turning out odd, unpalatable messes that made Plum's stomach flutter. Allison could whip up lovely meals when she was in the mood, but mood struck her so seldom that it seemed wise for Plum to take charge in the kitchen, deferring to Allison's cookery whims as they arose.

Plum watched as Tommy gave a few final swipes with the chamois, then stood back to gaze critically at the car for signs of imperfection. "Your lunch is ready, Tommy." She had made him a hefty bacon, lettuce, and tomato sandwich. Her boys had loved BLTs. And homemade sugar cookies and milk and an apple. A nice wholesome lunch. That young man needed some wholesome food in him, and Plum had delighted in providing it all week long.

She settled in with a cup of tea at the kitchen table across from him. She'd been careful not to pry, but Tommy would be leaving soon and she was very curious about him so, with kindly transparency, she began asking questions.

Tommy, sizing up his audience, obligingly spun a poignant tale of an Army officer father killed in Vietnam, a school teacher mother killed in a car crash when he was ten. He was adopted, he said, by a wealthy rancher who abused him physically, emotionally, and—dramatic pause—in *other* ways. Tommy confessed that he'd run away at fifteen and been running ever since. His greatest regret was that he'd never had a normal home life, never had an opportunity for a good education.

Plum, predictably, was touched by this tale. She thought

of her own four sons who had received lavish quantities of love and opportunities, and who had turned out so well. All except Jamie, of course, who had been killed in the same war that had claimed Tommy's father. Life was sometimes so sad. She wished there was something she could do for Tommy.

Tommy made no attempt to tug at the heartstrings of the other two women. With innate cunning, he knew that Jane and Allison would not so readily accept his fabricated biography. If, as was likely, Plum related the story to them, the other women might be skeptical but would imagine that Plum had embroidered the tale. And, if confronted, Tommy could deal with it. Anyway, he liked the spice of confrontation.

It came sooner than he expected.

Although fragile old ligaments heal slowly, Dr. Woodring pronounced Allison's recovery remarkable and saw no reason why she could not resume driving to the village, cheerily cautioning her, however, against entering the Indy 500. Just to be on the safe side, the women stocked in extra food, and Jane declared herself quite capable of walking the distance to the village for mail if Allison didn't feel like driving. This they thoroughly discussed before calling Tommy into the house in the late afternoon toward the end of his second week with them. Plum insisted they give him a twenty-five dollar bonus because he'd so faithfully served them, and it was she who made a pretty speech of dismissal.

Tommy listened impassively, then raised his peculiar yellow eyes. Gone was the look of polite acquiescence, replaced by a calculating gaze and an insolent smile. "Well, now, that's not quite what I had in mind, ladies. You see, I'm not moving on. I'm moving *in.*"

Chapter 5

"WHAT DID HE SAY?" Plum's hearing was not as reliable as it used to be. "He's moving in? Why, I don't believe there's enough room for him."

Allison, like a dog that bristles its fur to appear more threatening, stood taller. "Young man, your attitude—"

"Sit down, Mrs. Moffitt." Humorless yellow eyes met faded brown eyes.

Allison wavered only momentarily, then sat down.

Tommy insolently put his foot on the polished cherrywood table which had belonged to Allison's grandmother. He leaned forward to drape his arm casually over the hiked knee and stuck his other hand in the back pocket of his jeans. He looked cool. "I'd like to tell you ladies a little story. One of you already knows it, but you'll listen anyway."

"Tommy, if you'd just take your foot off that nice table—"

He glared at Plum. "Hey, lady, I'm talking."

"It's all right, Plum. The table doesn't matter." It had sunk in on Allison that Tommy Weed was serious. And quite probably dangerous.

"Okay. Here's the story. Once upon a time there was this nice lady, super respectable, y'know? And, anyway, she murdered somebody in cold blood. Now the question is this: which one of you nice ladies would I be talking about?" He looked at them, enjoying himself enormously. "I'll give you a hint. She murdered her husband."

"This is shocking, Tommy!"

"You're shocked, are you, Miss Plum? Let's see now, your husband—how did he die?"

"My husband died of a heart attack."

"So you say."

"Please, I beg of you, don't do this, Tommy." Big tears spilled from Plum's eyes and rolled down her soft pink cheeks.

"Don't start that crying stuff, you hear? We'll come back to you." He swiveled his body a quarter turn to Allison. "Maybe the most likely candidate would be the one with the longest string of husbands, right? What happened to all those husbands of yours, Mrs. Moffitt?"

Allison might have been carved in stone.

Tommy, who liked a challenge, slowly righted himself from his pose, walked over to Allison, and grabbed her left hand. "All those pretty rings. All those husbands," he said softly. "Do you want me to break your other wrist?"

"No."

"Then you tell me what happened to all your husbands, Allison, baby."

"You are despicable!"

Still smiling, Tommy began slowly twisting Allison's wrist until she cried out. "Now you tell me about those husbands."

"All right. Let go of me."

He straightened, smiling. "Tell us a story now. Take your time, we aren't going anywhere. What happened to those husbands of yours?"

When Allison was a child she had suffered through many a battle of wills with her overbearing father. Then, as now, she'd submitted to the other's superior strength while stoically maintaining her self-possession. She spoke levelly. "My first husband was Robert Nichols. We eloped when I was very young. Later the marriage was annulled and I never saw him again. He died a few years later."

"Of a broken heart?" Tommy gave a derisive laugh.

"Of a ruptured appendix," said Allison briskly. "My second husband was Franklin Ashmore. He was killed in the Battle of Casino during World War Two. My third husband was Roger Wyatt. He was an alcoholic, I divorced him, he re-married and died the following year of cirrhosis of the liver. My last husband was J.P. Moffitt who died two years ago of cancer. My husbands may not have died peacefully, but none died by my hand."

"And you survived them all?"

"I am a survivor, Mr. Weed." Their eyes locked: two survivors about to engage in battle. Tommy's glance dropped first. He turned abruptly to Jane.

"So we're left with plain Jane Browne. How did your husband die?"

Jane's face was drained of color, and she looked sick. "He died in an accident."

"Oh, an accident. A car wreck? A plane crash? Maybe a building fell on top of him. Huh? Huh?"

"No."

"How did he die? What kind of accident?"

"He was killed."

"Killed?"

"Shot to death."

"Shot to death?"

"By an intruder, a burglar."

"Really?"

"Please—"

"You shot him, plain Jane Browne. You shot your husband and I know it." This was the moment Tommy had waited for. All those months of patient tracking, of searching through old records, of asking questions, of hunting. That was the work, this was the fun, the pay-off.

"Let me tell you how I come to have that little piece of interesting information. Way back, before I was born, my father, who never had a lucky break in his whole life, knew a lot about surviving, just like ol' Allison there. Now my old man was self-employed, you might say. He collected things that other people weren't using. Silverware and stuff like that. He was an entrepreneur, you might say. He'd go into people's houses and he'd take what they weren't using and he'd sell it. He'd take from the rich to support the poor, mainly his own poor self.

"Well, one night he made a house call in a fancy neighborhood, thinking the family was gone because it was all dark. He pried open the back door and made his way inside, quiet as a cat. Well, it nearly scared the hell out of him when he walked into the living room and right there, sitting in the dark, was this man, big as life, but half asleep. Well, my old man tried to ease himself out of the house but the guy suddenly woke up and jumped out of his chair and started yelling and cursing at him. Then out of nowhere came the guy's wife, barefoot, wearing a nightgown and carrying this gun. And the guy kept yelling 'Gimme the gun, gimme the gun, you idiot!' And that's what she did. She gave him the gun. Yes, sir, she shot that bastard right between the eyes. And she watched him fall to the floor, just stood there staring at her husband who was dead as a doornail. Then she looked up at my old man. He thought sure she was going to kill him, too, but she just stood there staring at him, so he ran like hell out of there."

Tommy Weed had played his scene before a rapt audience. Allison and Plum gazed at him in disbelief. Jane sat rigidly, her face drained of color, her fingers locked onto the arms of the chair.

Tommy continued. "Well, the next day, my old man read in the paper a front page story about this prominent citizen, Dr. Logan Browne, who'd been shot with his own gun by an intruder. There was a picture of the poor widow crying her eyes out, with her little boy at her side. Real heartbreaking. All my old man could think of at the time was that the police were going to get him for murder and who'd believe he didn't do it? His word against that of a rich doctor's wife? He got out of town as fast as he could. Well, he got himself into a little trouble and ended up as the guest of the state of California for quite a while and, what with one thing and another, he forgot all about this murder he'd witnessed.

"I never saw my old man till he lay dying. I guess, in a

way, he was trying to impress me by telling me all the stuff he'd done in his life. And when he told me about this lady who had murdered her own husband right before his eyes, I got to thinking that justice hadn't been done. That lady killed somebody and got off free as a bird while my old man suffered mental anguish thinking he was going to be accused of something he didn't do. So it seems to me like there's an old debt owed to my old man. He's not here to collect it. But I am."

"What do you want?"

"No, Allison, this isn't your affair," Jane said. "I'll handle it. What is it that you want?"

"Money."

"I have very little money."

"Your doctor husband had plenty."

"That's true. It's also true that it all went to provide for my son's care and education. I never used a dime of it for myself."

"Well, I'm thinking that about fifty thou would square us up."

Jane couldn't help herself; she laughed out loud. "Young man, I don't have fifty thousand dollars. I'm retired, I get a modest little pension. That's what I live on."

"What about your son?"

"Well, of course, you can ask him, if you want. He's with a medical unit in east Africa. I'm afraid he gets paid mostly in livestock, however."

"Oh, shit."

"Yes, well—" Jane shrugged.

"Goddammit, you've got to have some money. You all have money!" He glared at Allison, the most conspicuous consumer of the trio.

"You can't blackmail me, young man. I didn't do anything. Besides, my attorney handles all my financial transactions. He'd have you behind bars in ten minutes if you approached him with this scheme." Allison never trusted anyone with control over her money, but she guessed that

Tommy was ignorant of such matters, and she'd no intention of giving him so much as a dollar beyond what he'd earned.

"What about you?"

Plum's eyes watered again. "Oh, dear, my boys take care of all my money and they would be ever so upset with your proposal, I'm afraid."

"My friends owe you nothing, young man." Jane had regained some of her composure. "I admit to no truth in your outrageous story, but I do have five hundred dollars in a savings account—"

"Jane!"

"No, Allison, I'm willing to give that money to Mr. Weed. He can go away and make something of himself. If he feels that his father was in any way wronged, he won't believe any denial from me anyway. I want to do this, Allison, and in exchange, Tommy Weed, I'd like you to promise that you'll go away and never bother us again."

Tommy pondered. "Okay, you've got it. Give me the money."

"I don't have any cash on hand and I doubt that you'd take a check. The bank is closed. You'll just have to wait till tomorrow."

"Sure, and you'll call the police in the meantime."

"No. However bizarre your allegations, I don't want to have those painful old memories brought up again. I give you my word, I will not contact the police. Nor will my friends."

Tommy understood finally that this was the best deal he was likely to cut. "Okay, but I'm staying here tonight. I'll be your guest."

Jane and Plum looked doubtfully at the owner of the house.

"Very well," agreed Allison reluctantly. "You'll leave as soon as you get the money in the morning and that will be the end of our association."

Unfortunately, she was dead wrong about that.

Chapter 6

IT WAS TOMMY'S experience in life that things just never worked out the way they were supposed to. Here he was all set to terrorize Jane Browne, and she was supposed to cave in and give him money so he could finally be somebody. It had seemed simple enough to Tommy, but then most things did at the outset. Instead, Jane had turned out to be practically broke, and her son was some kind of do-gooder doctor getting paid in goats. It was the story of his life and depressing as hell.

He'd sat morosely through dinner while the old biddies chattered away about politics and the potential success of a new village art center, just as if he hadn't been trying to extort money from them two hours earlier. Then, incredibly, they had left the table and gone into the living room to watch some screechy opera on public television. He couldn't stand it. He switched the TV off decisively and the women watched, puzzled, as Pagliacci shrank and disappeared into grayness.

"Bedtime, ladies."

"But it's just past nine o'clock," objected Jane.

"I'll make up the sofa for you." Plum stuffed her crocheting away in her sewing bag. She didn't care for Pagliacci. Such a sad man.

Tommy was furious. The way things were going, they'd probably want to tuck him into bed with nightie-night kisses.

"Hold it. I'm not sleeping on any goddamned sofa."

"It's quite comfortable really," Plum assured him.

"I'm gonna sleep in a real bed."

"We don't have an extra bedroom, Mr. Weed."

"Then I'll just look over what's available and take my pick. Two of you can double up."

He herded them into the north wing and when he saw Allison's sumptuous chamber, he gasped and put it in the only context he'd gleaned from the re-runs of old movies.

"Geez, it looks like a madam's bedroom."

"I beg your pardon?"

"Nothing. This room will be okay."

It was settled that Allison would share Plum's fussy bedroom; Jane would be in her own room alone. After Allison silently gathered up her toiletries and night-clothes, Tommy accompanied her into exile.

"What in hell do you think you're doing?"

Plum, puzzled, put down the bedside phone that had been covered by a doll in a hooped skirt.

"Why, I'm calling for the correct time to set my clock, the way I do every night."

It was hard to tell who was more furious, Allison or Tommy. They might at least have had the option of phoning the police if Plum hadn't been such a creature of habit or if she'd kept her wits about her and waited until they were alone. Why couldn't Plum *think?*

"Gimme that." Tommy unplugged the phone angrily. "I'm gonna lock this door so you won't give me any trouble. You've all got your own bathrooms, so you've got no need to get out till morning. Now, stay put. You—" He jabbed a finger at Allison. "You're going to have some broken bones if I have any trouble from anybody, understand?"

He locked the door, marched into Jane's room, grabbed the telephone there and, without a word, locked her in also.

He made a search of the house and found that the only other telephone was in the kitchen, resting primly in a built-in drop leaf desk. He pawed through the pigeon holes and found little of interest—bills, recipes, stamps. He also found several dollars which he pocketed, and a key. Lifting the drop leaf upright, he saw it had a sturdy lock set in the satiny wood. Trust ol' Allison to protect a collection of utility bills and petty cash with a strong lock. Grinning, he closed the desk and locked it. It amused him to think of the phone ringing away inside the desk and the old ladies unable to get at it. "When I split tomorrow," he thought maliciously, "I'll take the key with me." And he stuck it in his pocket.

Having finally rid himself of the ladies' company and severed their link to the outside world, Tommy didn't know quite what to do with himself. He sprawled out on the sofa and looked around the room. Nice place, he thought. Only if it was his, he wouldn't want all this antique junk. Too fussy-female. It could use a few neon beer signs. Yeah, that would spruce it up. He flipped on the TV, switching channels rapidly, pausing to watch a car chase sequence. When it ended in a fiery crash, he punched the off button. He looked around the room again. Books, magazines, all crap. He wished he had a *Playboy*. He lit a cigarette.

What he needed was a beer.

He went into the kitchen. The refrigerator was filled with carefully wrapped food and covered dishes. Beverages. Ah, here we go. Skim milk, tonic water, diet Coke, prune juice. Geez! What a collection. And no beer.

Restlessly, he strolled into Allison's bedroom. This was one hell of a room. There was something unsettling about an old lady surrounding herself with all this sensuous stuff—silk and brocade and downy comforters and deep carpeting. The ambience of the room was definitely arousing. Tommy thought of *Playboy* again.

What he really needed was a woman.

Stealthily he went through the house turning out the lights. He gathered up the phones he'd taken from the women's bedrooms, including Allison's, then locked up the house and went out to the garage. The Mercedes was waiting. He opened its trunk and dumped the phones in. The only telephone left now in the house was the one in the kitchen, safely locked away where the ladies couldn't get at it.

He had a plan. The availability of the Mercedes was too tempting. He'd go out and have himself a few beers, maybe get lucky with some woman. He thought of Allison's sensuous bedroom.

Hot damn!

"Shhhh—" Tommy waggled his fingers conspiratorially in the young woman's face and she giggled. They were both pleasantly drunk. "We don't want to wake my aunties, so shh—"

Her name was Tiffany Sims, and he'd met her in the bar of the Seafarer. It was not the kind of bar Tommy usually frequented, but the Mercedes lent him confidence. Tommy wasn't the sort of guy Tiffany usually let pick her up, but the Mercedes and allusion to rich relatives had endowed him with an appeal that he lacked physically. Tiffany liked conspiracy, and she had some floaty romantic notions of seduction within earshot of straightlaced old ladies.

They crept into Crooked House through the kitchen door, and on tiptoe Tommy led the way to Allison's bedroom. When he turned on the bedside lamp Tiffany gasped, just as he had done earlier.

"My God! What a layout!" she whispered in awe.

Tommy flopped down on the bed. "Com'ere."

"No, I want to look around first. My God!" She ran her fingers reverently over the rich brocade of the chaise.

"Com'ere," he called, louder this time.

"Shhhh. Don't get over-anxious, lover. I want to look at all this." She slid onto the chaise and struck a seductive pose. Was this luxury or what?

"Goddammit, com'ere!" Tommy shouted.

"Mr. Weed? What's going on there, Mr. Weed?" Allison's voice was clear and piercing.

Tiffany froze. "Why is she calling you Mr. Weed? I thought you said you lived with your aunts."

"Shut up, honey. It's all right."

"Mr. Weed, I want to know what's going on in my house. You unlock this door immediately."

"Why have you got her locked up? I don't like this."

Tiffany leaped from the chaise as though it were boobytrapped.

"It's a game, that's all. Come on, honey. Com'ere. Pay no attention. She's senile, she calls me crazy names, forgets who I am. They're all senile."

Tiffany had removed her shoes to enter the house. Now she hopped about on one foot, replacing first one, then the other. "I'm going home."

"No, no, it's okay, baby—"

"There's something weird going on here." She had her shoes on now. Tiffany liked a few laughs, but she was no dummy. Something was definitely strange here. And this guy was sounding like a real creep. There was no law saying a creep couldn't drive a Mercedes. "I'm getting out of here," she told him and marched resolutely out the bedroom door.

Tommy followed, cursing. In the darkened living room, he could make out her wiggly little body picking its way around unfamiliar furniture.

"Come back, baby—"

"Get away from me, you creep."

A wild rage throbbed in Tommy's head. He never got anything he wanted, never. Not money, not women, not anything. Women, they were always thwarting him. He grabbed her roughly, excitement flowing through him as she resisted.

"Stop it, you're hurting me. Let me go!"

Tommy heard the fear replacing anger in her voice. He hit her hard. She was a tiny young woman and she flew off her feet at the blow like a surprised butterfly, then landed, not lightly, but with a brutal cracking sound.

Tommy lunged, fell, capturing her with his own body. He laughed malevolently.

"Ha, gotcha! You wanted to be caught, didn't you? You like the excitement of the chase, huh? Hey, baby. Hey—" She did not struggle against him. He took her face in one hand and shook her head from side to side. "Hey, don't pass out on me, baby. We got things to do, you and me. Come on, don't do this to horny ol' Tommy. Wake up, baby."

He gave her a whack across the face. She didn't respond.

"Damn!" Tommy stumbled over to the nearest lamp, furiously struggled with the switch, cursing his own befuddlement, cursing Tiffany. Light flooded the room. Bright red blood festooned Tiffany's yellow hair and she stared in unblinking disbelief at the sharp edge of the marble-topped table against which she'd struck her head.

Allison stood by the bedroom door, breathless, listening hard over the rising wind and rain. She'd heard the voices, the sounds of footsteps through the living room, then the crash. The silence in the house now was most disturbing of all.

"What do you think is happening?" whispered Plum, who was sitting up in bed, clutching the covers to her bosom as if for protection.

"I don't know."

"Do you think he has someone with him?"

"He did have. Perhaps she left."

"That is *not* a nice young man," Plum concluded. "I'll be glad when he's gone." She was sorely disappointed in young Tommy Weed.

A moment later Allison heard Tommy's footsteps in the hallway and she drew back from the door. The key fumbled in the lock. Tommy cursed, tried again, then flung the door open. He looked disheveled and he stank of beer.

"We got us a problem. Come on out here."

The three women stared uncomprehendingly at the rag doll body of Tiffany Sims sprawled, unladylike, on the carpet. Words failed Allison.

But not Plum. "Oh, dear, whatever is that poor thing doing there?"

"It was an accident," snarled Tommy, immediately defensive. "She fell in the dark and hit her head on the corner of that goddamned marble table."

"But why was she here at all?"

"Plum!"

"Oh, dear—"

"Are you sure she's dead?" asked Jane practically. Hope fluttered through Tommy briefly, though he knew his own propensity for terrible luck.

Jane knelt down and felt the young woman's neck for a pulse, gazing intently at the still body as if to will life into it. After a moment, she rose and shook her head.

"Oh, the poor thing—" Plum cried.

"Never mind that. You gotta help me get rid of her. It was an accident, see? We'll take her down on the beach, like it happened there. It's all the same anyway. She fell here, but she could have fallen on the beach."

The women looked at him mutely.

"Go get dressed. You gotta help me."

"Mr. Weed, we must call the police," said Allison. "If, as you say, this poor young woman died accidentally, you won't be held responsible. She really deserves better than being left abandoned on the beach."

"Listen, lady, she don't know the difference. It was an accident, like I said, but who's gonna believe that? The cops will want to know what I was doing here. You think when we explain how I was trying to put the squeeze on you for money they won't think I killed her?"

"You've been working here," said Allison reasonably. "Everybody in the village knows that. We'll just explain that we offered you a place to stay overnight."

"That's what you say now. The minute the cops get here, you'll change your story."

"You have my word."

"No good."

"Then you leave here. And we'll notify the police after you've had a chance to get away."

"Sure, and they'll be right behind me. They'll know I killed her if I run away. Look, I got no wheels, I got no money. I'll have to have the money. My mind's made up. We dump her on the beach. Now, you go get dressed, all of you. I need help. *Move!*"

Tommy could easily have carried Tiffany Sims' body to the beach by himself except for the wooden stairs which were steep, narrow, and overgrown by salal bushes. And except for the storm which had broken about the same time Tiffany had departed the earth. He sent Plum and Allison down the stairs first to hold flashlights on the steps. He watched impatiently as they tentatively hobbled down the steps, clinging to the railing, their raincoats whipping mercilessly in the high wind. Jane, who was the youngest and strongest of the women, and for whom he held a grudge anyway, was selected to help carry the body.

His first thought had been merely to dump Tiffany on the sand, to get her out of his sight. The stinging rain seemed to have invigorated him; now he thought burial at sea was a better idea. She could have been wading and fainted or something, he thought. A bump on the head of a drowning victim might go unnoticed. Besides, it might take days for the body to wash up, and it might reappear miles from here. That would take the heat off him. Anyway, by then he'd be long gone, with Jane's five hundred bucks in his pocket.

They stopped for breath at the base of the stairs. Plum was sniffling, whether from exertion or the rain or grief, Tommy neither knew nor cared. He scooped up Tiffany's body in his arms. Thank God she was light. He sent the old ladies with their torches before him, acolytes for the priest of power who bore a sacrifice for the angry ocean.

"Okay, shine the lights on the water."

"Why?"

"She's going for a little swim."

"Mr. Weed!" The horror in Allison's voice evaporated in the wind.

"*Do it!*"

He waded out waist deep into the cold roiling water and shoved Tiffany Sims out to sea, waiting a moment to find out what would happen. It was hard to tell. She seemed to be sinking. He gave her a hard push. Ah, now she was outward bound. The rain lashed at him, the wind twisted through his hair. It didn't matter. He was powerful; he'd met this challenge cunningly. Satisfied, he turned and, breathing hard, waded back to shore. Two lights beckoned him in. A third bounced hurriedly toward the stairs. It was Jane.

He sprinted after her, still feeling his own power—nothing could stop him. They were weak, he was strong. He caught Jane just as she reached the stairs. Tommy had never played football, but he executed a neat tackle. Jane went down flat on her stomach with a loud "Ooof!" and he straddled her, the wild hard rain beating down on them without mercy.

"You thought you'd get away from me, didn't you?" He pushed her face furiously into the sand, hating her, hating his own bad luck that dogged his every step and had from the moment he was born. "Don't you ever try to cross me again. Do you hear? *Do you hear me?*" He pulled her face up from the sand by the hair. "Answer!" The power surged through his body. Jane might have been his despised mother or the stupid silly Tiffany. Women were conniving bitches, all of them.

Jane spat sand and nodded.

"I'm the boss, you hear? And don't you forget it. Not for a minute. If they get me for murder—which I did not do—then they'll get you, too. And the others as accessories. We're in this together. Understand?"

Jane understood. Perfectly well.

Allison helped Jane to her feet. To her surprise, Jane was crying. Never, in all the years she'd known Jane, had Allison seen her shed a tear. Weak, that's what they all were. Weak and helpless and dominated and humiliated by the likes of this dreadful young hoodlum. Plum was crying, Jane was crying. Well, Allison wouldn't give him the satisfaction of her tears. She stumbled on the last step and Tommy roughly jerked her forward. "Hurry up, you ol' bag of bones."

Allison still didn't cry, but she had to fight not to. An old bag of bones. That's what she was, what they all were. Old, old, old . . . .

Chapter 7

SIX WEEKS AGO on her forty-fourth birthday, Emily Bertram had taken off all her clothes, stood before the full-length mirror in her bedroom and burst into tears. She'd once been a pretty little thing, "no bigger'n a minute," Bert used to say. And now just look at her—a good thirty pounds overweight, flabby thighs, saggy breasts, pouchy stomach, rolls of fat quivering from her upper arms. Middle-aged human wreckage, that's what she was.

Not that Bert would ever say a word. Maybe he hadn't even noticed the creeping poundage. Bert's strength and his weakness were one: he accepted things. If he bid on a construction job and didn't get it, he just went right out and found another project; if he built something that was not exactly right, he dismantled it and started over. And if his wife looked like a balloon with feet, he loved her all the same.

Acceptance was well enough for Bert but not for Emily, not when it was her body that was bulging and sagging. She had marched down to Sea Sprite Square and bought herself a birthday present: a bright pink jogging outfit and a pair of gray Nikes with a sassy pink stripe. She walked a mile that first morning, feeling idiotic, a middle-aged pink rolypoly; she was sure she'd die of heart failure before she made it back home. When she didn't, she continued her walking until she reached a kind of lope, then she ran a little distance. Now she was up to a three-mile daily fast walk/slow run. She didn't know how much weight she'd lost and didn't want to know. Dr. Woodring told her not to weigh herself; muscle weighs more than fat, and she'd just be discouraged by revelations on the scales. Instead she looked at the results in the mirror. She was most definitely making progress.

Bert hadn't said a word. He had, naturally, just accepted the replacement of red meat, chocolate cake, and cream with offerings of fish, fruit, and skim milk. And she'd observed him, more than once, looking at her reflectively, as if wondering what she was doing different with her hair style.

Emily ran on the beach at dawn every morning in pale sunlight or fog, in mist or rain. What had once been a loathsome chore was now an invigorating beginning to her day. She knew the beach as well as she knew her own back yard, so when she spotted the blob at water's edge that morning, she knew it was something new that had washed ashore in the night. She thought it was too large for a tangle of seaweed; possibly it was a dead seal. She jogged along placidly, drawing closer to the thing which was too green for seaweed or seal. Something plastic maybe.

A lot of things got abandoned on the beach. Nature herself threw from the waters dead or dying whales and seals, fish, birds, crabs, seaweed, driftwood, and shells. Humans abandoned trashier stuff—plastic bottles, shoes, cans, towels, toys—and sometimes other humans.

Emily's pink-clad arms and legs churned forward rhythmically, then halted abruptly.

"Oh, Lord," breathed Emily. "Oh, Lord—it's a *person!*"

Each of the women at Crooked House had her own style of beginning a new day. Allison was fond of sleeping late and rarely rose before ten. She woke slowly, sometimes listening to music, sometimes switching on radio news reports if she felt masochistic; more often she would read, or get the pen and yellow lined pad from her bedside table and make lists of things to do or to instruct others to do. Only after a leisurely awakening was she ready to emerge from her comfortable cocoon.

Plum was a cheery morning person, and she didn't mind being cheery by herself. She dawdled over dressing, hair preparation, and tidying her room before leaving it for the kitchen which she liked having to herself. She pottered leisurely, making something tasty for her breakfast, cleaning up afterwards, humming half-forgotten hymns from her southern Methodist childhood, planning meals for the coming day. Then she would tiptoe into the living room, settling herself into her chair to catch whatever was left of morning shows on television.

Jane liked to rise early, eager to begin her day. She brewed her tea and poured a bowl of granola which she took, squirrel-like, back to her room to munch on as she wrote down the previous night's dreams and then began work on her poetry.

This morning was different. Jane woke up in great discomfort, having spent the night bunched up on the chaise in Allison's bedroom. When they'd come up from their grisly mission on the beach last night, Tommy had relinquished all claim to this room, declaring instead that he'd take over Jane's space. She suspected the truth, that Tommy's amorous advances had been repulsed in here, and he didn't care to revisit the scene of his humiliation.

Where she slept was the least of Jane's concerns. She had been appalled yesterday afternoon when Tommy had begun recounting the story of murder; it had been like hearing someone tell the plot of a movie she'd seen long ago and had half forgotten. It was in the re-telling that the setting, the facial expressions, the gestures, the voices had sprung suddenly to life.

Those memories had been painfully vivid when she'd met Plum, and through her, Allison, a year after Logan's death. By then Jane had perfected a way of saying that she was widowed with such finality that few people pressed beyond that stark statement, and the few who did received only an icy gaze in response. But in Plum she had seen an accepting confidante and had, in time, described the official version of Logan's murder which, to her surprise, Plum had known all along. Plum's husband was, after all, part of the judicial system and would have heard his colleagues gossiping about the case. It had never been mentioned again in all these long years, and Jane doubted that Plum ever even told Allison.

Jane shifted on the narrow chaise and wished she had her notebook so that she could record her dreams and work on her poetry. Lord knew how long she'd be imprisoned here; Allison might well sleep till noon.

Tommy should be up soon, though; he was eager enough to get out of here. Of course, if he wanted that money he'd have to wait till she could get to the bank when it opened mid-morning. She sighed. What a predicament. It didn't matter about the money. Jane never worried about money anyway. She had enough, and her needs were simple.

They might all say, in hindsight, that they hadn't trusted Tommy Weed, but for Jane this was accurate. She'd detected from the outset a slyness in him and, worse, a suppressed rage, which to their collective peril she'd ignored. She knew from years of association that Plum trusted virtually everybody and Allison virtually nobody, rendering them both poor judges of people.

She wondered about that poor creature who'd died here last night. Tommy had forced Jane to help carry the young woman's body, and she remembered with remorseful clarity those thin legs and high-arched feet. Poor thing, just out for a good time and, like Plum, all too willing to trust. When Tommy had carried the body to the sea, Jane had seen an opportunity to run for help. She remembered the humiliation she'd felt when he'd caught up with her, dragging her down, pushing her face into the sand. She'd always thought of herself as strong and agile. She once was. Last night on the beach she'd forgotten that she was old.

Yes, she was old and it no longer mattered what Tommy Weed told the police about Logan's death. It would be uncomfortable, but it would not be devastating. She'd lived too long at peace with herself to be undone now. Let Tommy talk.

What she could not do was to let him get away with the

murder of that young woman. She had no idea how to stop him. And there was no way of knowing when or where Tiffany's body would wash ashore.

When Emily Bertram excitedly telephoned the local police to report finding a body on the beach, it was the deputy, Lep Younger, who took the call.

Lep had played football at Oregon State until he'd exhausted his eligibility. Like many another collegiate athlete, he had misunderstood his primary purpose at the university and was startled to discover that the failing grades he'd systematically accumulated, despite intensive tutoring and summer term attendance, had resulted in his dismissal from the halls of learning. He had imagined, erroneously, that his mentors—coaches, well-heeled alums, and faint-hearted members of academic committees charged with the admission and retention of students—would endlessly pull strings to keep him in school and thus on the playing field, which was the treatment he'd received since he first joined organized sports at age ten. Unfortunately, Lep just wasn't good enough for the string-pullers to shield him from reality indefinitely. So he'd left the university pretty much as he'd entered it, academically unenlightened, with rah-rah still ringing in his ears. The old boys' network, which devoted itself to the nurture of college athletes, filling their pockets with cash, buying them clothing, cars and other necessities, wasn't much interested in a has-been football player. A few agreed to make an inquiry or two and eventually someone called in a favor from Conrad Snyder up in Windom, asking him to hire this deserving young lad. Con had obligingly put Lep—he'd been known as The Leopard on the high school gridiron—to work at one of his construction enterprises. Lep was a strapping fellow, well over six feet, with huge shoulders and the neck of a bull. Unfortunately there were other, less flattering bovine comparisons to be made above the neck as well, and Con cast around quickly for another

occupation that Lep might be suited to before he did some
real damage to the building trade.

Windom had just hired a woman as police chief, and
Conrad figured that if equal opportunity were to be meted
out to females it might as well also be given to the academically inept. Con called in a few favors himself, and Lep
Younger was hired as a deputy police officer.

And he certainly did cut a splendid figure in his uniform,
though Con blanched a bit when he realized they'd issued
Lep a firearm. Still, he reassured himself, nothing much ever
happened in Windom. The kid could strut around looking
like a serious upholder of law and order, scaring away the
freaks and the weirdos.

Con never dreamed Lep would be called upon to investigate a murder. But it was Lep who responded to Emily
Bertram's summons, and with siren wailing and tires
screeching he arrived at the scene of the crime. All the
commotion naturally alerted the strollers, joggers, and even
a group of Chinese tourists performing T'ai Chi on the
beach, that something extraordinary was happening. All
flocked to the scene.

The siren woke the late sleepers on Rich Row, too.

It woke Tommy Weed who rolled out of bed, remembered
the events of the previous evening, and stumbled to the
window to look down on the beach.

Lep Younger, tall and godlike in his uniform of authority,
stood out from the crowd.

He was gazing up at Crooked House.

Chapter 8

TOMMY, AS BEFITTED his paranoid personality, panicked easily. He lost no time in routing the women out of bed, lining them up in a bedraggled row on the sofa, and demanded answers to his questions.

"They've found the body. What am I gonna do? How am I gonna get out of here? Where am I gonna get money?"

"When the bank opens—"

"I can't wait for the goddamned bank to open! How much money have you got here?"

"Well, let's see now—" Plum put a prim finger to her lips as an aid to calculation. "I believe I have twenty-seven dollars. No. No, I bought stamps day before yesterday. Or was that last week?"

"Never mind. Say twenty bucks." He looked at Jane.

"Three or four dollars. Six, seven. I don't know. You can have it all."

"You've got money." Tommy directed this flat statement like an accusation at Allison.

Now Allison was a wealthy woman, and she didn't get that way by throwing dollar bills out the window. She spared no expense on those things that she wanted or felt she was entitled to have; she was often moved to generosity by friendship or familial ties or good service; she gave graciously to such charities she deemed worthy. If a thief ordered her at gun point to empty her pockets she'd have done so without hesitation. But to be asked by this impertinent young man to disclose her cash resources and meekly turn them over to him called forth an obstinacy usually reserved for the Internal

Revenue Service. Allison had pink satin pockets sewn into every bra she owned and in those she always carried a folded hundred-dollar bill everywhere she went, be it Hong Kong or the corner grocery. She also had five twenty-dollar bills hidden in her bedroom (three in books with dull titles unlikely to appeal to borrowers, one under the paper liner of a box of handkerchiefs someone had given her thirty years ago, and another in the bottom of a decorative jar of cotton balls). She viewed these as emergency caches, used them rarely and then systematically, beginning with the bill between the pages of *Arachnids of the Northwest*. It was her habit promptly to replace whichever of these bills she'd spent in an emergency.

She said to Tommy, "I have thirty-two dollars and some change in my purse." She did not actually offer it to him.

"Maybe fifty bucks between the lot of you. Fifty lousy bucks."

"We don't keep much cash on hand, Mr. Weed. Clearly it isn't safe for elderly women to do so."

The irony went past him. "How far can I get on fifty lousy bucks?"

Jane answered him realistically. "Not very far, I'm afraid. If you can wait until the bank opens, I've promised you five hundred. You can have it, as I said before, if you'll just leave us alone." If she could just get to the bank, perhaps she could get help. She felt responsible for Tommy being here. He didn't have a weapon; he couldn't very well strangle her in the middle of Citizen's Village Bank, could he? It was their only chance to get this loathsome young man apprehended.

"Okay, okay, I've got no choice but to wait."

"That's settled, then," said Plum pleasantly. "Let's have a nice breakfast, then you can be on your way."

Chief of police Chris Kirksey had grown up in Windom but had left it to go to college, grateful to escape the insular inquisitiveness and the smothering solicitude of village life. She had returned fifteen years later with a diploma, a divorce decree, a daughter to support, and a dawning realization that if you really couldn't go home again, but you tried to anyway, they'd still love you there. And they'd still be aggravatingly inquisitive and smotheringly solicitous. They'd also find you a job and be encouraging that even though you'd never been a police officer they had all the faith in the world that you could learn.

And so she had. A year after her hiring, when the then-chief of police had died in the line of duty (felled by a heat stroke while directing Fourth of July traffic) the villagers had said well, why not make Chris the chief because by now she'd had some training under The Best (God rest his soul) and some experience with Windom's problems, and anyway, how demanding could it be in a little coastal resort village where the major problems were summer traffic snarls, high-spirited drunks, and juvenile vandals? And so she had assumed the duties of chief and had run the law enforcement department as well as had her predecessor, God rest his soul.

Naturally, as in all human endeavors, there were problems. Chris did not like her deputy, Lep Younger. He was spoiled, accustomed to getting by on his brawn and his boyish manner. He did not understand, although he was twenty-six years old, that life was not one big football game. She could have forgiven him this naiveté. In a sense, Lep was a victim of a system which rewarded such young men for being good at playing adolescent games and postponing the business of growing up. What she deplored was his unpuncturable air of superiority. She could not look at him without recalling Thurber's description of another athlete: "While he was not dumber than an ox, he wasn't any smarter." If only, occasionally, Lep could make a clean, honest declaration of "I don't know" instead of covering up with defensiveness, crude language, or guffaws.

When Chris had been appointed chief, she had objected to hiring Lep as her replacement. Con Snyder, however, was a sufficiently powerful figure on the Village Council to ram through the appointment of this former football hero. Chris

needed her job and philosophically decided that she would
find a way to work with Lep. She had enough brains for
them both and he had enough brawn. It was not an ideal
arrangement, but it seemed to be one she'd have to learn to
live with. It proved difficult. Lep was like a little kid playing
cops and robbers, seeing everything in simplistic good guy/
bad guy terms. Where Chris used low-key communication,
Lep used muscle. Shortly after he was hired, she'd had a
nightmare in which Lep had cautioned a jaywalker on the
village main street, then shouted "Freeze!" and assumed the
squat two-handed firing position against the hapless wrong-
doer. She'd waked up before he could pull the trigger.

No, Chris did not like Lep, did not like his swaggering
and his bragging. Nor did his patronizing attitude toward
her ease their working relationship. Predictably, Lep viewed
women, as he'd once informed her, as "good in only two
places—the kitchen and the bedroom." Wink, wink. She
fully understood that he was not sufficiently secure with
himself to be able to work under the direction of a woman,
and this understanding often, but not always, strengthened
her tolerance.

Lep phoned Chris to report the discovery of Tiffany Sims'
body on the beach. He might have been reporting a half-
million dollar federal grant, so high was his excitement.
"Hey, Chris, guess what! We got us a dead body—maybe a
murder!"

Sharply at ten that Wednesday morning the Mercedes pulled
up in front of the Citizen's Village Bank. Tommy left the
motor running and turned to the back seat where Jane sat,
pale and shocked.

"You understand what you're to do?"

"Yes."

He made sure by reiteration. "You withdraw the money.
You say nothing to nobody. No tricks. If you try anything
cute, I drive off with Allison here and you'll never see her
alive again. I promise you that, understand?"

"Yes."

"Okay. Go!"

Allison, sitting erect and furious next to Tommy, watched Jane disappear into the bank. Jane would not try to ask for help, not after they'd watched Tommy lash Plum to her rocking chair and gag her with a lacy camisole. Not after they'd seen the expression on his face as he reveled in his own power over Plum, tightening the bonds with unnecessary force, grinning when she winced under his rough handling.

Allison was incensed. She was accustomed to being in control, to giving instructions, not following them. She did not care for the role of victim. She glanced at the odious Tommy hunched over the steering wheel, staring nervously at the door of the bank as if he expected Jane to emerge any moment leading a pack of armed troopers. He was scared and that, in Allison's view, made him explosive.

Jane came out of the bank. She was wearing a hideously ugly orange pants outfit with a bright green purse dangling from her shoulder. At least no potential witness was likely to forget seeing her. As she climbed into the back seat of the car, Tommy asked, "Did you get it? The whole five hundred?"

"Yes."

"No tricks?"

"Certainly not."

"Okay. No, don't give it to me yet." He'd caught sight of Nedry Jarvis' suspicious face peering out one of the bank windows. Tommy couldn't know that Jarvis' all-occasion facial expression was disgruntlement and did not denote curiosity about Jane Browne's withdrawal or what she intended to do with it. Jarvis disapproved of people in general and people who made withdrawals in particular. Still, Tommy didn't want to be seen receiving a packet of money. He pulled out onto the main street and circled the block.

"Where are we going?" asked Allison.

"Portland."

"Then what?"

"That's for me to know and for you to guess, so shut up about it."

"What about Plum?"

"She'll be all right."

"Mr. Weed, Plum is sixty-eight years old. You simply cannot leave her tied to a chair all day long."

"She'll be okay. She's tough as nails. You all are." There was a hint of admiration in his voice; they *were* tough old broads, all of them. "We're going to stop for gas. Behave yourselves, now."

The attendant began to fill the gas tank, gazing dreamily off into the distance.

"Do you want to put this on your credit card, Mrs. Moffitt?" asked Tommy politely, loud enough to reach the ears of the young man who was now lethargically swiping at the windshield.

Allison gave Tommy a venomous glare but dug into her purse for the card. Maybe when she signed it she could write HELP! instead of her name. She weighed the odds of Tommy not seeing the message against the attendant's likelihood of understanding it. No. Tommy was far sharper than the sluggish-looking attendant. It wasn't worth the risk. Besides there was poor Plum to consider.

When the fellow moved away to record the transaction, Tommy said to Jane, "Okay, gimme the money." She handed it over and Tommy stuffed the bills into his pocket without counting them. "It better be all there."

"It's all there."

"Good morning, Mrs. Moffitt."

Bert had pulled up in his pick-up on the other side of the pumps adjacent to the Mercedes. Allison's heart leaped hopefully at the sight of the contractor.

"Good morning, Mr. Bertram." She could feel the ripple of tenseness emanating from Tommy. He switched on the ignition and the Mercedes purred into idle.

"You're up early." Bert, like villagers everywhere, followed a precise interactive ritual based on the assumption that the business of every inhabitant was to be placed in a common pot, stirred up occasionally, and freely dispensed to feed the hunger of curiosity. Allison felt a flutter of gratitude for the casual inquisitiveness of the residents of Windom but before she could extend the conversation, Tommy pressed ferociously on the accelerator and they took off abruptly, leaving Bert to stare after them.

"Nice try, lady."

"What do you mean?"

"You yammering with the guy back there at the gas station."

"His name is Mr. Bertram and he'd have thought it odd if I hadn't spoken to him."

"Yeah, you're clever, Allison baby. You better watch it or you're gonna get your clever self killed."

Tommy turned off onto the Portland road. He was driving very fast.

"Mr. Weed, I'd like it if you wouldn't drive so fast."

"Mrs. Moffitt, I'd like it if you'd shut your face."

The beautiful scenery of the coastal mountain range flew past them unappreciated. After a few moments, Allison spoke again. "What will happen when we get to Portland?"

"Never mind. I got a plan."

Allison doubted it. Tommy might have some half-developed scheme but he was essentially an improviser, had probably learned to be through necessity.

They had gone no more than ten miles when they rounded a curve and came upon a line of stopped vehicles. Up ahead they could see the whirling blue lights of a state patrol car.

"Geez, a roadblock! Well, they won't stop me!"

He demonstrated his ability to improvise by making a sharp U-turn and heading back toward Windom.

Allison breathed a long sigh, grateful that Plum hadn't been a passenger, for she would surely have felt moved to correct Tommy's error and kindly point out the sign he'd failed to notice advising motorists that the road ahead had washed out, closing one lane of traffic.

The state patrol was there on other business.

Nobody was looking for Tommy at all.

Chapter 9

LEP YOUNGER STUFFED the last of his three lunch sandwiches into his mouth. He wadded up the paper wrapping and gave it an agile toss into the wastebasket.

"Two points!" He grinned exuberantly at Chris.

She gave him an impatient look. "Please get on with your report." She had long since given up requiring Lep to submit written reports on any matter of importance; she'd been appalled at his first barely literate efforts. Two years of college, and he could hardly decipher the collected works of Dr. Seuss.

"Okay, so anyway, Tiffany's boss said she was good at her work, didn't goof off, was very friendly to the customers—with an emphasis on *very* when it came to male customers." The villagers' penchant for keeping track of one another's business made it relatively easy to reassemble the public mosaic of Tiffany Sims' last night. Tiffany had worked as a waitress at the Harbor Inn for about a year, as did her roommate, a young woman named Candy Ann Lester. Lep continued, "She worked her usual shift last night. Seemed the same as always, left about eight-thirty, as usual. She and Candy Ann then went up to Seafarer's bar where they liked to go to drink and dance. And pick up guys."

"Did Tiffany ever try to pick you up?"

Lep gave Chris a salacious wink. "Look at this beautiful body. Of course she did."

Chris looked sorry she'd asked.

Lep didn't understand Chris Kirksey. Take most women now, he got along fine with them. Joke around, give 'em the ol' eye and they melted like butter under the attention. Not Chris. She always looked slightly disgusted with him, and Lep had no idea why. It wasn't like she was some kind of dried-up old prune face. She wasn't that old, late thirties, he judged, but hell, he'd had women that age. Fell all over him, they being in their sexual prime (or so the guys in the locker room had informed him) and he being just slightly past his, although there was certainly nothing to worry about in *that* department, not for the ol' stud.

Ol' stud. Yeah, probably all Chrissy needed was a man. He studied her, expertly assessing her physical superstructure. Great body, he concluded, not for the first time. Probably passionate as hell in the ol' sackeroo. Yeah, she was probably one of those gals who would take some convincing that she really wanted it. A flash of fantasy unreeled in his head: Chris struggling against him, clad only in one of those lacy brief things women wore. The idea excited him.

She punctured the fantasy incisively. "So what did you find out at the Seafarer?"

"Oh. Well, Tiffany and Candy Ann had a couple of glasses of wine. There were some college kids there, staying in one of the condos and they decided to move the party to more private quarters." Wink, wink. "Candy Ann joined them but Tiffany had hooked up with some guy. Candy Ann didn't know him, but I think maybe I've got a line on him. A coupla guys I know were at the Seafarer, checking out the action, and they saw Tiffany with this guy. Mid-twenties, slight build, nothing special. Probably a jerk. They've seen him around town the last week or so, having a beer at the Blue Dolphin, just hanging out, y'know, walking around town. I checked with Dolph and he remembered seeing this guy but doesn't know who he is. Thought maybe Bert might know, but he wasn't home. I'll check him out later."

"Sorry to interrupt." Conrad Snyder did not look sorry. He looked like a man with a mission which he fully intended to pursue.

Chris gave him a perfunctory nod and Lep said, "Hi, there, Con—how's it goin'?"

Conrad Snyder was in his early forties, good looking in a bland made-for-TV kind of way. He savored his role as big man in the little town of Windom. His manicured fingers were in many entrepreneurial pies, the Seafarer condo complex and the Sea Sprite Square among them. Con placed a high value on being a winner; he radiated self-confidence like strong after-shave lotion.

He had opposed the appointment of Chris to chief of police ("I've got nothing against women, but . . . "). When other voices prevailed in her promotion to chief, Con did not waste time on fruitless recriminations. He smilingly mended fences and flagged the Kirksey file in his memory bank: one of these days he'd get rid of her.

"I just heard of the death of one of our young people," he said mournfully.

"You must have been out of town, Con. The body was discovered early this morning," observed Chris affably. They all knew how fast news traveled in the village. Con Snyder had undoubtedly heard of the discovery within a half hour—and probably from Lep Younger.

"It looks like foul play." Lep liked jargon.

"Foul play," Con repeated, with little tsk-tsking sounds underscoring the phrase. "Well, it won't do for Windom to be seen as a place where foul play is tolerated."

"You want me to put her back in the water, Con? Maybe she'll float down to Newport."

"This is serious, Lep." Con's voice was sternly reproving. Lacking a reliable sense of humor himself, he was never quite sure when others were joking. "What I mean is that we have to make the best of this bad business. And we do that by showing how skillfully we can rise to the occasion with our first-rate police crew." He glared meaningfully at the primary crew members who sat before him.

Lep responded to the pep talk; he was accustomed to being urged into glorious battle by a father-figure.

Chris merely sighed at this belaboring of the obvious. "We're conducting an investigation, Con, and rising skillfully to the occasion."

"Listen, missy, you better rise swiftly. I'm thinking of calling an emergency meeting of the Village Council tonight and you better get this cleared up quick or your job just may be on the line."

Chris leaned back in her chair. "I talked to the county medical examiner a while ago. Tiffany Sims was dead when she went into the water. She died from a blow to the head, not drowning."

"So we have got us a murder!" Lep grinned and struck the heels of his hands together. He was ready to go out on the field and fight, fight, fight.

"There's no way of knowing that for sure at this point," said Chris, moved to contrariness by Lep's enthusiasm. "She could have been on the beach and fallen, hitting her head on something. We see a lot of accidents around here. When a body washes up on the beach there's a good chance it was somebody with one drink too many who was doing something foolish. All we have to go on now is the preliminary report from the M.E.'s office. The purpose of the investigation is to determine how Tiffany Sims died and under what circumstances."

Chris' display of calm irritated Conrad Snyder. When serious situations—like a threat to business—occurred, he wanted to see some excited reactions. "You know what a thing like this could do to Windom, don't you? It could be a severe economic blow to us all. People aren't going to come here to relax if there are dead bodies cluttering up the beach, if they think they'll be attacked by some maniac."

"I think you're getting a little ahead of yourself here, Con."

"I want to see some action!" He brought a fist down on the desk. It was a theatrical gesture which riveted Lep into edge-of-chair attention.

Chris shrugged. "I could ask the U.S. Navy to shell the beach, but I don't see how that would help."

"Okay, sassy lady, be flippant." Con waggled a finger at her. "But if I don't see results pretty damned quick, you're going to be collecting unemployment checks."

When Tommy had tied her to the rocking chair, Plum had meekly submitted. She'd sat quietly, listening to the key turn in the lock of her bedroom door and to the noisy exit of the three (Allison loudly protesting Plum's bondage); she'd heard the crunch of the Mercedes's tires on the gravel drive, and then only the ocean's repetitive roar and the seagulls' cries.

She tested the gag, still embarrassed that Tommy had grabbed this very personal garment (her camisole!) for the purpose of ensuring her silence. He'd used her nylons (and a *good* pair, too) to secure her hands behind her, knotted through the chair slats, then tied her feet together with another pair of nylons. She really wished he'd used her everyday stockings for tying.

She also wished she'd asked him to turn on the radio before he left. She hoped he'd come back before dark; he hadn't left a lamp on either. She decided not to think about the long hours between now and nightfall.

Well, if you're in a locked room, tied up with your own underwear and you can't get loose, and you're apt to be there for a while, the thing to do is make the best of it. And that meant amusing yourself to make the time pass quickly.

The first thing Plum thought of was Clovis. She had a naive view of life-after-death and often pictured her late husband as a white-robed winged angel flying around the heavens with a small harp tucked carelessly under one arm (Clovis had not been musical) and a cigar clenched between his teeth. If Clovis were looking down at her predicament right now, he would be highly displeased.

It made her sad to think of her deceased husband, so she thought instead of Jane's deceased husband. She had never told Jane, but Plum had long known that Logan Browne's reputation was none too saintly. She doubted that *he* was flying around heaven in angel garb with her Clovis. If

Tommy's wild tale were to be believed and Jane had indeed shot Logan Browne, it had quite possibly been by accident. It was all so long ago. Jane was her friend and a good woman. Plum could neither judge nor blame her for what might have happened all those years ago.

She thought of Tiffany, that pitiful young woman who had died in this house. Plum probably wouldn't have cared for Tiffany if she'd known the living person, but she'd have found something pleasantly acceptable about her—a nice smile or a pretty figure, for it was Plum's way to see good in people. Why, she'd even seen good in that wretched Tommy. She knew now that the story he'd told her of his early life was a lie; that the true story was probably far more painful. An unloved, unwanted little boy—what a high price is paid in this world for children who are brought into it unwanted. Poor Tommy. . . .

After a while, Plum cast about for something else to help the time pass. Heavens, she might be here all day. Poetry. Poetry had the power to soothe, like the sea. As a young schoolgirl, Plum had been required to memorize and recite passages of poetry in class, standing straight and enunciating clearly, trying to avoid the eyes of giggling schoolmates. She'd joined the others in decrying the uselessness of memorization, yet secretly she'd enjoyed it. And it surprised her, over the years, how often she'd call to mind those memorized lines.

"Let me not to the marriage of true minds admit impediments . . ."

Da da da da . . . what came next?

She was in the midst of her third sonnet ("When in disgrace with fortune and men's eyes, I all alone beweep my outcast state . . .") when she heard Allison's clarion command: "Mr. Weed, I insist you open that door immediately!"

Well. They hadn't been gone till dark after all, thought Plum, and she'd survived quite nicely.

Chapter 10

ALLISON MADE A light lunch for them all, despite Plum's protestations that she was perfectly able and quite willing to resume her place in the kitchen. There was, as Plum knew, no point at all in objecting when Allison insisted upon assuming a caretaking role. It did not descend often, fortunately, and Plum bore this gruff nurturing patiently, hoping it would soon subside.

After lunch, Allison sent Plum off for a nap with the same logic she'd used in child-rearing: Mother's cold, put on your sweater; Mother's exhausted, you go take a nap. It had worked well enough with the children, they'd turned out quite all right. And if she'd warped their psyches, well, what were mothers for? She'd done as well as she could, untrained as she was for the job of motherhood. Allison did not waste time on regrets.

She went to her own room, sank down on her bed, closed her eyes, and attempted to turn off her racing mind. Tommy had been strangely silent since they'd turned back at the cautionary road block, and his silence had a brooding quality that Allison didn't like. Undoubtedly he felt trapped. And that might be very dangerous. He had the money now. Maybe she should just tell him that the road had been washed out, not blockaded by police searching for him. She'd give him the car and he could drive off. He'd have to lock them up in a bedroom, of course, while he escaped, she quite understood that, but surely they could attract attention in time and be rescued. Yes, that's what she would do, tell him—just as soon as she had rested.

It was late in the afternoon when Allison woke. The house was quiet. Wouldn't it be wonderful if Tommy had stolen the car and driven off while they'd napped? But of course he hadn't, for he still believed the roads were blocked and the police were looking for him. She got out of bed, reaching for her cane. Her arthritic knee was acting up again. Probably due to the stress. She hobbled out of her bedroom, the deep carpet muffling her footsteps.

Tommy sat dozing at the kitchen table, his hand loosely caressing a mean-looking butcher knife. Allison bought only the very best cutlery; that knife could cleanly cleave a chicken bone. Even if she could grab it without waking him, she likely could not keep him at bay. He was young and agile and she was neither.

Could she get to the phone? All she'd have to do was punch out 911. Then what? Scream her name out? No, there wouldn't be time enough. Her breathing had become shallow as she reflected on her alternatives, which seemed severely limited. Could she perhaps make it to the front door and run outside, screaming for help? She saw herself creeping toward the door on tiptoe, wrestling with the door latch, pulling open the door. No, no, it was not possible.

She thought, "I could whack him over the head with my cane, grab the knife, and—"

"What are you looking at?" Tommy's eyes opened suddenly, his hand grasping the knife more firmly, and his voice held a frighteningly vicious note.

Stiffly, Allison sat down at the table across from him, using her cane to lower herself into the chair. She arranged herself carefully, then looked directly at him. "Mr. Weed, there wasn't a police blockade on the highway this morning. The road was washed out after the storm last night. No one is looking for you on the highways."

"How do you know?"

"I saw a sign on the road, cautioning a washed-out area."

"Sure, and you just now thought of it, right?"

"No, I didn't tell you at the time because I was worried about Plum being tied up here."

"She was okay."

"But I didn't know that."

"I told you she'd be all right, didn't I?"

"Yes, you did."

"And now you want me to believe I can get in that car and drive off to Portland and nobody will stop me? You think I'm stupid, lady?"

"No, I think you're a very cunning young man, actually. I also think you're anxious to leave here. I'm telling you that there was no road block this morning, that parts of the highway were washed out after the storm, and that apparently the police were there to direct traffic while the road crew was setting up a temporary bypass. Or possibly there had been some minor accident because of the washed-out road. I really don't know. It had nothing to do with you."

He looked at her and nervously fingered the knife handle, weighing the degree of trust he felt. He was desperate to take action, to get out of this place, away from these chattering women. He pondered.

The front door chime galvanized him. He darted to the kitchen window with the quick and agile movement of an animal.

"Goddammit, the police!" He gave Allison a venomous look. "Trust you, right?"

"It's probably a routine—"

"Shut up!" He pushed her roughly down the hall to Jane's bedroom. Jane sat at her desk absorbed in verse writing. Tommy yanked her to her feet and put the knife at her throat.

"Walk!" He dragged Jane toward Plum's room. "Me and plain Jane here are going into this room with the other old lady. You are going to tell the police that you don't know anything about anything. And if you try to get cute, try to give any kind of signal, I will cut their throats. Both of them. I'll be watching you every minute. Do you understand?"

"Yes."
"I'll kill them both, lady!"
Gazing into his glittering eyes, she did not doubt it.

Allison was reared in an era when police officers generally
received respect and admiration. They were seen as friendly,
helpful, brave, and courteous, like grown-up Boy Scouts. She
knew the modern-day cynicism aimed at police, the view
that they were corrupt, brutal, power-hungry. She had not
been around for seventy years without observing a consis-
tency in human nature and knew those simpler days had
likely not been so idyllic. Still, she much preferred viewing
the police as protectors rather than as compromised
upholders of the laws they enforced. She realized when she
opened the front door that she'd anticipated seeing a strong
young man. Instead there stood a golden-haired woman in a
sharply pressed khaki uniform. She looked attractive, com-
petent, and confident. She did not look like someone who
could kick open a door and rescue two hostages from a
malevolent killer.
"Mrs. Moffitt? I'm Chris Kirksey of the Windom Police.
May I come in?"
"Yes, of course." Allison admitted the policewoman readily, motioned her to a comfortable chair, and thought about
Tommy listening and watching from the bedroom. As they
seated themselves, Allison noted the holstered gun on Chris'
hip and weighed that weapon against the knife at Jane's
throat. It was no contest.
"Mrs. Moffitt, the body of a local woman was found on
the beach early this morning in front of your house here.
Perhaps you've heard the news?"
"No. No, I haven't been out today. I hadn't heard."
"I'm visiting all the homeowners in this area to see if they
might have seen or heard anything last night that might be
helpful to our investigation."
"I sleep very soundly, I'm afraid."

"Perhaps you knew the dead woman. Her name was Tiffany Sims. She was a waitress at Harbor Inn."

"No, I've never dined there." A waitress, that's what that pathetic little creature had been. And she had died in this room, a few feet from where Chris Kirksey now sat. Allison shuddered, recalling how last night she and Plum had cleaned up the blood of Tommy's victim from the marble table and the patterned carpet. If only they hadn't been so thorough.

She brought her attention back to Chris Kirksey, who was holding out a photograph. "I have a picture of her, it's fairly recent. If you'd just look at it, please—"

Allison took it reluctantly, held it at arm's length, then quickly brought it closer. Her glasses were in the bedroom and she dared not fetch them. She gazed at the blur that was Tiffany Sims' likeness. "No, I'm sorry. I don't know her."

"You've never seen her then?"

When it suited her, Allison could tell a bald-face lie without hesitation. Generally, and certainly under the present circumstances, she would prefer veracity. "I may have seen her. I can't say positively."

"Have you noticed any strangers about here?"

"Well, I'm something of a stranger here myself, so it's hard to say. And then with all the tourists here—" Allison shrugged helplessly and gave Chris Kirksey a nervous smile.

"I am thinking in particular of a young man, between twenty and thirty, medium height, rather slight of build, who has been around the village for a week or so."

Allison pretended to ponder, then said, "Such a vague description. I'm afraid I can't help you, no."

"I understand that you have two housemates, Mrs. Moffitt. Perhaps one of them might have seen—"

"They're resting. In fact, I just got up from a nap myself," she said quickly. There was an awkward silence. "I'll tell them what you've said, and if they've noticed anything they can telephone you." Allison rose, signifying an end to the interview. She did not believe she could sustain this awful charade another moment.

At the door, she felt a rush of panic. "Officer—"

"Yes?"

"Please, I—I'm sorry. Tell me your name again?"

"It's Chris Kirksey."

"Chris Kirksey. Yes, thank you for coming." She closed the door on hope, feeling like a kindergartener watching her mother leave on the first day of school with the dread of unknown horrors waiting.

Back in her office Chris made some notes on her afternoon's activities, then put aside her pen and gave herself over to reflection. The interviews with the residents of the houses along the beach front where Tiffany's body had been found proved unrewarding. The session with Allison Moffitt was particularly dissatisfying. Chris was a woman highly sensitive to the dynamics of personal interactions, to the spoken and unspoken messages which passed between people, to the currents and atmosphere of setting. Mrs. Moffitt had been nervous, unforthcoming, and had shown a remarkable lack of curiosity about a body on the beach. Her demeanor did not fit with the picture Chris had pieced together from casual observations and village tittletattle.

She turned her consideration to Tiffany Sims and the information she'd collected about her. It was not unusual for single young people to come to the coast to work in the summertime when resort jobs were plentiful, then to stay on into the winter as Tiffany and her roommate had done. After a while they moved on, or less likely, settled in the area. Tiffany was typical. She'd drifted into Windom last summer and got a waitress job. Her friends were the people she worked with; she liked to party, had never been in any trouble. She was friendly, paid her bills more or less on time, and was generally quite unremarkable.

The medical examiner, a cautious man, had been reluctant to say that Tiffany had been murdered. She had died instantly of a blow to her head such as might be received in a fall. She was already dead when she went into the water, but how she got there or how long it had been after she'd suffered the blow, he couldn't rightly say.

Chris glanced at her watch. It was after six and past time to leave for home. There was nothing more she could do today, she thought, indulging in a good stretch. She wondered if Conrad Snyder had managed to assemble the Village Council for a meeting tonight. If so, she clearly was not invited. It was possible, of course, that the other Council members balked at a formal meeting. They'd undoubtedly spent the day chewing over every morsel of available information on Tiffany's death. It did not surprise Chris that Con saw this as an opportunity to get rid of her. That had been on his agenda since the day she was hired.

It was getting on toward six-thirty when Chris pulled into her driveway. The beachfront cottage which she shared with her daughter, Carolina, was the house where she herself had grown up, where she'd returned in disillusionment when she had found the big wide world was not as wonderful as she'd imagined. She loved this welcoming cottage on the north end of Rich Row. It was unashamedly homey with a 1950s kind of innocence: an honest-to-God white picket fence (as her former husband had marveled when she'd brought him to Windom to meet her family), an arched rose trellis, a big shade tree, and Priscilla tie-back curtains at the windows. The house looked safe, warm, cheerful; a home where there was love and laughter and a sense of family. It had been that way when she was growing up here, although she had not truly appreciated how special it was. She had wanted desperately to recapture that sense of warmth and safeness when she'd returned here with Carolina. Did a single parent and a child constitute a family? Certainly they did, but there was an aching incompleteness.

There were days, and this was one of them, when Chris felt depressed with her life. A man should be driving up, home from work, not she. Chris should be opening the front

Mat, Mpaskowg-28

SURGICAL SHORT STAY UNIT (SSSU)

The afternoon before the day of
surgery, call 257-3611 ext. 4809
to find out what time you are to
report to the SSSU. Call between
3:00 & 4:00 P.M., if Monday surgery
please call Friday.

On the day of surgery, use the new
Community Wing entrance, take the
elevator (left) to the second floor
Turn right and pass the SURGICAL
SERVICES sign. Proceed to SURGICAL
SHORT STAY sign. Enter the waiting
room & report to the Nurses'Station
in SSSU.

Please report to the following
Departments, which have been (✓),
for Pre-testing.

LAB____ RADIOLOGY____ EKG____

OTHER____

ANESTHESIA____ If there is a che
here, please stop at the Anesthesi
office which is next to the Cashie

When Pre-testing is done on Sat.,
call Anesthesia ext. 4675 Monday
thru Friday 9:00 A.M. to 4:00 P.M.

door to him, waving, drying her hands on a frilly scrap of apron, exchanging an embrace. A weary part of Chris cried out for that tender scene. A practical part of her gave a derisive laugh. Things never were as neatly simple as all that. Her ex-husband had usually returned home exhausted from the burden of breadwinning in a competitive academic jungle. And she'd never worn a frilly apron, had often felt numbed by repetitive housework, and had even been envious that he'd had the opportunity to use his mind and creative energy while she got to scrub the toilet.

In any case, she refused to look back in regret. She was now the breadwinner, with that glorious opportunity to use her mind and creative energy. It was she who got to deal with scintillating colleagues (like Lep?) and interesting people (like Con?). It was she who got to make her mark on the world: ejecting drunks from the Blue Dolphin, giving stern lectures to teenaged vandals, and filling out endless repetitious reports.

She parked the police car in front of the garage and greeted the German shepherd who pranced forward with delighted yips and wriggles of welcome. "Hello, Duchess." Chris put her key in the front door lock, realized there was no need for a key, scowled, and let herself in. The smell of supper beckoned from the kitchen.

"Carolina! I'm home!"

"Hi, Mom."

"The door wasn't locked."

"Oops, sorry."

Chris gave her daughter a quick kiss which Carolina adeptly shrugged away. "I don't want you to be sorry, I want you to be safe. Keep the door locked, okay?"

"Oh, Mom, it's not like we live in Chicago. This is Windom. Nobody locks doors in Windom."

"We'll be trend setters, then. It's important to me. Keep the door locked."

"Why? I've got Duchess for protection."

"Lock the doors."

"Okay, okay." Carolina decided not to use door-locking as a vehicle for self-assertion. "Dinner's ready. You want to eat now or do you want to unwind?"

"I'm more hungry than tired."

"Oh, good. You're going to love this dinner, Mom."

Carolina was a throwback to her grandmother, whose culinary talent was legendary. When they'd returned to Windom and Chris had gone to work, Carolina had wandered into the kitchen and found belongingness. She had a gift for cooking that Chris thought must be like having perfect pitch; Carolina simply knew how to combine ingredients and produce excellence. Chris sometimes felt guilty that her child was saddled with such responsibilities, but whenever her cup of guilt reached the running-over stage and she offered to make a meal Carolina would say with matter-of-fact accuracy, "No, no, I do it better."

Carolina at fifteen was an unfinished replica of her mother. They both had big dark eyes the color of sable and heavy rich gold hair. Chris was tall and Carolina was rapidly catching up to her height. Most of the time Carolina was delighted that she so closely resembled her mother, but at other times when she wanted or needed to declare her separateness or when she felt critical of her appearance, she would rage against this physical inheritance.

Carolina had concocted a country French casserole for dinner—eggs, fresh mushrooms, bits of fish baked in a white wine sauce. They customarily ate in the dining room at a round table, both seated so that they could look out at the ocean. In her absence from Windom, it was this mealtime view, this daily reminder of the sea, that Chris had missed the most.

"I heard that Tiffany Sims got killed. Do you like the casserole?"

"Yes, it's delicious. Yes, Tiffany Sims was killed."

"Did you have to look at her, identify her body or anything?" Carolina took a bite of salad.

"Not at the table, please—"

"Sorry. Ghoulish, huh?"

"Yes."

"Well, anyway, what I heard was that she was raped and bludgeoned and thrown into the ocean."

"What you heard was rumor. She wasn't raped, she died of a head injury. We don't know yet how it got there."

"There's all sorts of talk going around the village, like how there's this crazed rapist on the loose and no female is safe."

"And still you didn't lock the door?"

Tommy unlocked the front door at Crooked House and stepped out into the night air. He'd secured the old ladies in two bedrooms and turned out all the lights in the house. It was a still and moonless night. On the beach below he could see several flickering driftwood fires. He wondered if he could risk a walk on the beach. It was dark. Likely the people on the beach were tourists, strangers here like himself, people on vacation and oblivious to local news of murder.

Tommy could not have identified his own feelings if he'd been asked what they were. Loneliness, for him, was ever present. He'd never belonged anywhere, never felt a part of any group. He'd been a nuisance to his mother, always in her way, as she'd been quick to let him know. He'd never belonged at school, always had felt puzzled at the expectations teachers seemed to have of him; he did not believe that he was dumb, simply that nobody ever had troubled to explain to him what it was that he was supposed to do, or how to do it. The rules that governed his life were vague and unfathomable. In this, he had more in common with Allison Moffitt than either of them might have guessed.

So there had always been the loneliness, covering him like a foggy shroud. It had been with him so long now that it was a part of him, unexamined and unquestioned, like his yellow eyes and crooked teeth.

But there was something beyond loneliness; it was a

yearning. He wanted something, yearned passionately for something. And he knew not what, only recognized the symptoms. He wanted power over something so that he might feel real. Wanted to be able to demand what he needed, so others would be so fearful that they'd see that he got it. He wanted freedom. He wanted to be able to go where he pleased. On Tuesday he could have done that, did do that. Now it was Wednesday and he was a prisoner. And that was his life: Tuesday he had a plan, Wednesday he was thwarted, and he struggled and cursed until it was Tuesday again and he had another plan.

In the darkness of the beach he could see the line of whitecaps where the water rushed in to shore. He did not think of Tiffany Sims who was now dead; he felt neither guilt nor pity toward her, only rage that she had spoiled his plans.

It was her fault.

Oh, she'd been pretty though.

Power and freedom and a good-looking woman. . .

He closed the front door behind him and walked softly into the dark night.

Carolina had watched TV for a while, then gone to her room to listen to music, clearly audible in the living room where Chris was reading. Chris felt contentment now, the depression of her homecoming having lifted. She was glad she was single, glad there were just the two of them in the house. There was a snugness tonight—each person knowing the other was there, but they were separate and being separate was agreeable. There would likely always be times when Chris would long for someone special in her life, for a man who was loving and sensitive. There were times when she also wished for a million tax-free dollars and for peace on earth.

Chris had been a dreamer, a romantic, and it had taken a few hard jolts in life for her to let go of some (certainly not all) of her dreamy romantic notions. She'd been the much-wanted child of elderly parents, living cozily among the gossipy villagers where she was known and loved as were most other children here, as if they were all common property of the villagers. She grew up under the watchful eyes of what amounted to an extended family. "Does your mother know you're doing that?" she heard often enough, or "Did your father say you could go there?"

It was still that way in Windom to a large extent. Everyone knew Carolina, knew that in summer she worked mornings at a day care center, knew she did the family cooking, knew who her friends were and how she got along at school. They knew, they cared. Chris was not overly concerned for Carolina's safety ordinarily; Carolina was level-headed and Windom was a safe place for youngsters. The death of Tiffany Sims was a harsh reminder that no place is completely safe.

Carolina was not a romantic as her mother was. Chris believed this came from the relationship, or lack thereof, with her father. Chris' ex-husband might be charitably described as an absent-minded professor. He undoubtedly loved his daughter but was preoccupied with his work, and now with a second marriage, stepchildren, academic tenure and upward mobility. He had little time for his daughter.

"Well, it's his loss," Carolina had finally concluded with a proud toss of her head. "He's missing a lot, not knowing who I am." Brave words that covered great pain.

There was nothing unique in this parent-child struggle, what the psychologists called the essence of the developmental task of children. Nice words that made it all seem so simple. It was not.

Chris put aside her book, yawning, and went upstairs. She looked in on Carolina who slept peacefully with Feather, the calico cat, snuggled up next to her rump and Duchess curled up on a rug at the foot of the bed.

*   *   *

At 12:30 Chris' bedside phone trilled. With one hand she lifted the receiver, with the other switched on the bedside lamp.

"Chris, this is Conrad Snyder."

"Yes, Con?"

"It's my daughter. It's Deb. Oh, God—"

"Con?"

"Chris, it's awful—"

"Please tell me what's happened."

"She was attacked. Someone tried to rape her on the beach tonight. He tore her clothes half off, pushed her into the water, tried to drown her, then dragged her off. Oh, God, it's awful."

"Is she okay?"

"Hell, no—but she's alive."

Chapter 11

THE IMPRESSIVE Snyder home hugged the crest of a hill north of town, commanding an unbroken view of the Pacific Ocean. There was no beach access, but the Snyders were not strollers by the sea. They were tidy people who liked to look at the ocean but did not care to have it come too close. It was too messy, too damp, too sandy, too salty. Nature, they believed, was best enjoyed at a snug distance.

Some day Deb Snyder would be attractive. At present she was fifteen and sulky, with a haircut that looked as if she'd done battle with a buzzsaw. She was huddled on an expensive blue floral-patterned sofa, wearing a bunchy white terrycloth robe, dabbing at her pink-rimmed eyes with tissues which she pulled from a box on the glass coffee table before her. At her feet was a collection of used tissues where she dropped them after wiping first her eyes, then her nose. Gloria Snyder, her mother, sat on a matching blue floral-patterned love seat with her own collection of tissues.

Conrad Snyder was neither sitting nor crying. He paced, a-quiver with outrage.

Chris sat down next to Deb on the sofa.

"Sounds like you've been through quite an ordeal tonight, Deb." Chris spoke gently. She was not in uniform but had pulled on a pair of jeans and a sweatshirt, hoping that the unofficial garb might appear reassuring to a youngster who'd been through a terrifying experience.

Deb nodded her head silently and turned the wad of tissue over and over in her hands.

"I need to know what happened. Could you tell me about it?"

Deb swallowed hard and nodded again. She shot a reluctant look at her parents but did not speak.

"Just take your time and tell it in your own way," Chris prompted. Silence. "Why don't you start with after dinner? You went to stay overnight at your friend's house—"

"Yeah."

"You went over to Barbie's?"

"Yeah. Me and Barbie and Steph were staying over there. Nothing special, y'know. Listening to music, talking and stuff. And we had a couple of movies to watch on the VCR, y'know?"

"So it was just an ordinary get-together?"

"Yeah." Deb spun the tissue wad a little faster. "And then—well, I don't know what happened exactly. We were having fun and then Barbie really started cutting me down. She does that sometimes, just really knows how to cut a person, and I finally just had enough of it—"

"Barbie, that little snot!" sputtered Conrad. "It's all her fault. If she weren't such a little snot—"

"Now, Con—"

Chris shot Deb's parents a restraining glance. "Go on, Deb."

"Well, anyway, I decided that I didn't need all that, didn't want to stay where I wasn't welcome—" She dropped the tissue into the pile on the floor, drew out a fresh one and cried into it with great self-pitying sobs. When the tears subsided, she continued, "So, anyway, I thought I'd just walk home along the beach, y'know? And I was walking along and thinking about stuff and then I realized there was this guy behind me, sort of, and he said something and I just walked on, faster, y'know? And then he said something like 'Hey, baby' and I started to turn around, then he—he grabbed me and he was saying stuff like 'Hey, baby. Hey, good looking.' And then he started tearing at my shirt and he tore it off me practically. I mean, it's *ruined!*"

Another barrage of tears, and two more tissues floated into
the pile at her feet. "And then we were sort of struggling and
he pushed me into the water and then started dragging me
over by a big pile of driftwood logs and pushed me down and
started trying to rip off my pants and I fought him like crazy.
He kept trying to kiss me and I couldn't scream and it was
just like one of those nightmares, y'know? Well, maybe he
heard something or got scared. Anyway, all of a sudden he
just got up and ran off. And I came home and told my
parents and they called you and that's all."

"And I want to know what you're going to do about it."
Conrad had held his silence to the bursting point. His fury
focused on Chris. "It's come to this, even in Windom, safest
place in the world, you'd think, to raise kids. Suddenly
there's some maniac running amok and attacking innocent
young girls. By God, I will not sit idly by and watch it
happen." He thumped the arm of his chair decisively and
jumped up again as if to prove his readiness for action.

"Con, I realize this is hard for you. I can fully empathize
with your anger. I need to get information before I can take
any action." Her calm seemed to deflect his anger momentarily. "Gloria, I could use some coffee right now. Con, why
don't you give Dr. Woodring a call? I think it would be a
good idea for the doctor to see Deb, make sure she's okay. In
any case, a mild tranquilizer might help her get through the
night."

Con's idea of action had been to form a lynching party or
at least to punch somebody in the nose, but he settled for
calling Dr. Woodring.

When Deb's parents left the room, Chris said, "Deb, I
need to ask you some specific questions and then we'll be
done. Are you up to that?"

"Yeah, I guess."

"You were walking north on the beach, is that right?"

"Yeah."

"Now where were you when the man first spoke to you?"
She thought for a moment. "I'm not sure."

"Past Crooked House?"

"I didn't notice exactly. Yeah, past Crooked House. That's where Tiffany Sims' body was found, right?"

"Yes."

"Yeah, well, it was somewhere in there, I guess."

"Did you notice this man before he spoke to you?"

"No, he was just, like, suddenly there, y'know?"

"Can you describe him?"

"Well, it was dark and I couldn't really see him."

"It was too dark to see his features, but perhaps you had a sense of his size or build."

"It was too dark." She concentrated hard. "Well, I think he was tallish, maybe. I don't know. Maybe average height. Average build, I guess. I don't know. I'm not good at noticing."

"What was he wearing?"

"I don't know. Jeans, maybe. Yeah, jeans and a shirt. Just clothes."

"Jacket?"

Pause. "No."

"Were any other people around?"

"No, not really. I mean, you know how it is on the beach. People may be walking but you don't pay attention to them. Or they may be sitting on logs, talking or something, but they seem pretty far away."

"Did you pass anyone? Or actually see people sitting on logs?"

"Not really. I just had an idea people were around, sort of. There usually are this time of year, but nobody close by."

"Where were you walking—on the wet sand fairly close to the water or back up nearer the hills where the houses are?"

"On the wet sand, pretty close to the water."

"The man spoke to you, you ignored him, then he spoke to you again and then he grabbed you?"

"Yeah."

"How did he grab you?"

"What do you mean?"

"Did he grab your arm or did he grab you around your waist?"

"He—let's see—he put his arms around me, like around my shoulders, and we sorta struggled and somehow he ripped my shirt. I mean, he was trying to rip my shirt, y'know? And then we struggled some more and he sorta dragged me into the water."

"Was he trying to drown you?"

"I don't know. We were just struggling around in the water. Then he started dragging me up toward the driftwood, like I said. And when we got there, he pushed me down and fell on top of me and he was trying to get my pants undone. And I was fighting him like crazy. He was trying to kiss me and stuff and I kept turning my head from side to side, like this." She demonstrated.

"Now, at this point, he was very close to you. Did you get any sense of facial distinctions?"

"What do you mean?"

"Well, was his face bearded, clean-shaven, stubbled? Was it smooth or pimply?"

"No. I mean, I don't know. I can't remember."

"What about smells?"

"Smells?"

"What did he smell like?"

She giggled. "I don't know."

"You may remember later. Smells are very powerful—things like tobacco, aftershave, alcohol, licorice, gum, sweat, bad breath, soap. Anything?"

Deb shook her head, intrigued by the range of human odors, none of which she'd noticed.

"So after some struggling, he let you go. Did you bite or scratch him, make any marks on him?"

"No, I was just hitting him, sort of."

"And you don't know why he gave up the attack and ran away?"

"No. He just did."

"Which way did he run?"

"I don't know. I was just crying and stuff. He left. I didn't pay any attention. I just got up and ran home."

"Did you see anyone on the beach at this time? As you were leaving?"

"No, I just ran. I just wanted to get home. I went up to the beach access road by the Seafarer and then walked straight home."

Dr. Woodring arrived to examine Deb. When they'd left the room, Chris accepted the cup of weak pale coffee Gloria Snyder had brewed. The clock on the mantel ticked with a mesmerizing rhythm as parents and policewoman sat together in the sterile, stylish living room. Chris wished she could think of something comforting to say but rejected as banal, "Deb's had a bad fright but it could have been worse."

Gloria said it, however.

Con topped her. "If I ever catch that bastard, I'll kill him!"

"I'll do the best I can," Chris promised, feeling sorry for him in his troubles.

"Your best better be good enough, missy."

"I'll see you tomorrow."

By eight o'clock the next morning the village hive was buzzing with the news of the attack on Conrad Snyder's daughter. Orin Brixby bustled out to sweep the sidewalk in front of his Gullway Market, and kept a sharp eye out for Fudgie Pike next door. Fudgie owned the neighboring candy store and was a regular on Orin's gossip exchange circuit. Orin knew about the attack on Deb Snyder because Paul Mercer, the paramedic, lived in the garage apartment on Orin's property; Paul also doubled as relief man for the police. Paul had been on duty last night, and he knew that Orin's morning greeting of "What's new?" was far from casual. Orin expected to know what fire, flood, pestilence or general mayhem had threatened the community whilst he'd slumbered. So Paul told him.

Fudgie Pike, who was thin as a pencil despite her fondness

for her own confections, arrived later than usual to open up her shop. Orin was fairly dancing with his broom in anticipation of imparting the choicest tidbit of information he'd had since the hippie candlemaker had run off with the mayor's wife.

"Did you hear about Con Snyder's girl?"

Fudgie could not possibly have heard. She spent her evenings in front of the TV soaking her bunioned feet, went to bed at ten, and rose just in time to get to the store by eight to supervise the candymaking before the shop opened for business at ten.

"No, what about her?"

Orin told the story he'd heard from Paul, supplying any missing details from his own imagination with the preface of "What I think is—"

And what Orin mostly thought was that there was a murderous monster on the loose in Windom. A ghoulish part of him wanted this to be true, for he did love excitement and there wasn't much to be had in Windom. A decent part of him hoped it was not true, and a conservative businessman part feared its economic damage. He saw all this reflected in the mirror of Fudgie's jellybean eyes.

Orin finished his news report and his sweeping simultaneously. He and Fudgie practiced a precise division of labor in their rumor-mongering. He would have the honor of delivering news to the locals as they came into the Gullway Market. It would be left to Fudgie to spread the word beyond their adjoining sidewalks. She knew her assignment and made haste to get her assistant started on the salt water taffy, then popped around the corner to Joe's little cafe.

Joe's Place catered reluctantly to tourists. Its location off the main strip of village businesses did not attract much off-the-street trade; you had to know the place was there. The locals knew. It was their secret refuge from the tourists, and they filled the horseshoe-shaped counter, leaving two lonely little window tables for whatever nonlocal traffic might wander in. Joe had hoped the plain name he'd chosen for his business would deflect tourists toward Sarah's Tea Cozy (gingham curtains, croissants, herbal teas and exotic coffee blends), or The Noodle (Italian menu, checked tableclothes, candles in wine bottles), or Harbor Inn (nautical motif and seafood). All these eateries were newer, far more attractive, higher priced, and their owners openly courted the tourists.

Joe did not court the tourists. He liked the business of the locals, liked being the hub of village life, saw his little cafe as a modern-day general store. Unfortunately the quality of his food—thick hamburgers and homemade french fries, chicken salad and open-faced crab sandwiches, and pies he made fresh daily himself—was such that word crept out and inevitably tourists ventured down the side street to the shabby little cafe. The locals ignored them, the service was stiffly courteous, and still they came. The locals did not mind presenting their village as cutely quaint, but most were reluctant to put themselves on display as cutely quaint natives. When it was time for them to gather and gossip and gripe, they wanted to do so in private and Joe's was the place where they wanted to do it.

Fudgie was greeted warmly when she entered Joe's Place, and her bony bottom had barely settled on the stool before she erupted with the hot news item of Deb Snyder's attack the night before. Her audience was bedazzled.

Everybody had an opinion except Joe, who wiped the countertops, refilled coffee cups and, like a good host, encouraged the flow of conversation.

Mr. Rainwater of the post office offered the opinion that the attacker was a sex maniac who was motivated by filth received through the U.S. mail in plain brown wrappers. Nedry Jarvis expressed the dour view that this was the work of cocaine dealers whose multimillion dollar enterprise was somehow being threatened by nubile young girls. Dolph, from the tavern, believed it was somehow a Communist conspiracy. Fudgie, upon reflection, suggested it might be the doings of some crazy religious cult members.

When their imaginations began to wind down, Joe asked how Conrad was taking all this.

"Hopping mad," was one accurate guess. "And I'll bet he's giving Chris Kirksey a hard time." As they'd all witnessed Conrad Snyder's virtuoso displays of temper, there was an awed moment of silence as they contemplated what acrimonious words might have passed between this leading citizen and the chief of police.

"He'll have her job if she doesn't arrest this lunatic pretty quick," Mr. Rainwater predicted, shaking his head sadly. He liked Chris.

"He never did think much of a woman police chief," sniffed Fudgie.

"Well, now, maybe he's right about that." Nedry Jarvis didn't think much of women in the workplace either. He would not allow his wife to work, no sir. She stayed at home where she belonged.

"Well, she'll sure be put to the test by all this," commented Fudgie, preparing to return to her candy store, her duty done. "She surely will be."

Usually Carolina was urged to ride her bike or walk to her morning job at the day care center because the exercise was good for her. Her teenaged attitude that adults were unfathomable was reinforced when her mother insisted upon driving her on Thursday morning.

"Why? Usually you won't give me a ride to work unless I have a temperature of a hundred and ten." Perversely, when she was offered transportation, Carolina preferred providing her own.

"Carolina, there was an attack on Deb Snyder last night."

"Was she raped?"

"No, thank God. She was roughed up but she's all right. However, just to be safe, I'm going to drive you to work. You can have lunch with me at Joe's Place." This Chris offered as a treat. Carolina was fond of Joe who freely dispensed cookery advice and regarded her as a protégée.

"And I want you to spend the afternoon at Emily Bertram's. I've already called her."

"Mom!" Carolina sang the word out in three protesting syllables.

"Sorry, Carolina. This is the way it has to be."

"I can take care of myself. I'm not a baby."

"I know." Theories of adolescent accomplishments of developmental tasks might fall easily from the pens of experts in slick magazines where Chris sought parental guidance, but in day-to-day practice, it was gritty stuff.

Carolina demonstrated this by punishing her mother with noisy preparations for departure, slamming drawers and doors while directing icy glares at this exasperating mother from whom she'd had the gross misfortune to be spawned. Chris sighed and did a quick mental calculation. Carolina was fifteen. Only five more years to go before teenagehood passed, like the measles but longer lasting. There were parental rumors holding that as early as seventeen some youngsters recovered from this affliction. With any luck at all Carolina might be one of them.

They rode together in the patrol car in frosty discomfort.

"I'll pick you up at noon and we'll go to Joe's for lunch."

With a frigid display of persecution, Carolina slammed the car door and stalked away toward the day care center.

From the office Chris phoned Dr. Woodring for a report on Deb Snyder. There wasn't much to go on: slight bruises on Deb's upper arms, no unusual bruises or swelling on mouth, face, neck or breasts. Apparently the attacker had either not been very strong or not very enthusiastic.

She spent a tedious hour with Barbie and Steph, Deb's friends, who were scared they were going to be blamed for Deb's decision to walk home by herself.

She spent an equally tedious ten minutes instructing Lep Younger to go to the state park and check out the campers there to see if anyone had seen or heard anything on the beach last night.

"Keep it friendly, Lep. These people aren't suspects. You're only after information, if they have any."

"Con's real upset over all this."

"Of course he is."

"He said he'd shoot the bastard if he caught him."

The less said about shooting in Lep's presence, the better. "Just go ask friendly questions in a pleasant manner. No shooting."

Before lunch, Chris went down on the beach to the area where Deb said the attack had occurred. She must have been badly confused or had completely misjudged the location. If she'd been walking near the water, as she said, and the tide was out, as it had been, then the nearest driftwood pile was well over a hundred yards away. That was a long distance to wrestle and drag a protesting victim.

The day care center where Carolina worked had been started the previous year by a young woman with a degree in early childhood development, two small children of her own, and an itch for a career. In the summer, when many of the locals worked full time and overtime, it was a boon for families with small children. Carolina had been hired as a trainee to assist the regular staff. In Windom most local youngsters worked in family enterprises, and Chris was grateful that while she could not provide her daughter with a summer job, others could. And did.

Carolina was still sulking when Chris picked her up for lunch. She flopped into the car and turned her head away from her mother to stare out the window in apparent fascination at scenery she saw every day of her life.

"I don't want to go to Joe's for lunch." Her announcement bristled with hostility.

"Okay. How about some yogurt? I'll stop by Gullway and pick up a couple of cartons and we can have a picnic on the beach."

"I despise yogurt," said Carolina. "I despise picnics, and I despise the beach."

Chris sighed and stopped at the Gullway, picked up two cartons of the despised yogurt and drove to the state park overlooking the despised beach. All the picnic tables had been claimed by tourists so Chris suggested they sit out on the grass to eat.

"No." Carolina preferred to sulk in the discomfort of the hot car.

"Fine." Silently they pulled the foil tops off their yogurt cups and dug in with plastic spoons.

"Look, Carolina—"

"I don't want to talk about it."

"It would help if you'd listen then."

"I can't stop you from talking." Carolina shrugged her shoulders insolently.

Chris hated these scenes with her daughter, mostly because one look at that pinched angry face brought forth a disconcerting memory of having played Carolina's role herself, feeling miserable and insulted by her own puny power. She'd not guessed, as a daughter, how tumultuous a mother's feelings were.

She took a deep breath. "I know you're upset that I'm asking you to go to Emily's this afternoon. You probably think that I'm being overly protective, and perhaps I am. I just have to risk your not liking me very much for a few days for doing what I believe is best for you. And I'm sorry."

"You're just overreacting."

"That's entirely possible." Chris looked out at the dancing blue Pacific. "I feel very unhappy about all this."

"Feelings, feelings! That's all you ever talk about." Carolina's voice lashed out in anger. "I *loathe* being treated like a baby."

Chris spooned the last of the yogurt into her mouth; it had the bitter taste of conflict. "I think you're bright and level-headed, Carolina. And I know you use good judgment. Windom's an unusual place. It's safe here, and we get lulled into feeling that nothing bad can happen in this village. And that's not true. When something awful does happen, parents like me feel scared. I wish I wasn't scared. I think having the run of the village has given you great self-confidence."

"But not enough, because the minute something happens that might test it, you reel me in on my leash and send me to a baby sitter."

"Emily's not a baby sitter and you aren't a baby. I can't allow you to be alone when there's a dangerous person on the loose. You're just too important to me. And that's the way it is."

"I'm certainly more level-headed than Deb Snyder."

Chris agreed, then asked curiously, "How level-headed is Deb Snyder?"

"Oh, Mom, she's so stupid. She does dumb stuff all the time. She's always chasing guys, always wanting to be the center of attention. She thinks she can do or say anything because her father's got money. She's totally disgusting."

"She sounds a little mixed-up, like somebody who tries too hard."

"That's what I'm saying, Mom, she doesn't *think*. Like going down on the beach late last night by herself. She probably got ticked at Barbie and Steph and decided to make some big dramatic gesture to get back at them. It never occurred to her that the beach wasn't too safe at that time of night for walking alone. But she'd just think of how dramatic it would seem to her friends if she disappeared for a while. She could have gotten Barbie's dad to drive her home or called her own parents. She didn't have to walk home, especially not along the beach. The road would have been shorter anyway."

"You don't like Deb?"

"Well, no, right now I don't like her. She did something stupid so I have to be treated like an infant."

Emily Bertram had prepared some chicken sandwiches on whole grain bread (without mayonnaise) with a fresh garden salad (without dressing), and hoped that Chris and Carolina would stay to lunch with her. It was easier to exert will power over calories in the presence of an admiring audience.

"Well, actually, I'd love to stay to lunch," said Chris gratefully. "We did stop off for some yogurt but that seemed only to whet my appetite."

Emily beamed, pulled out kitchen chairs for them and filled glasses with iced tea (without sugar).

"I heard about Deb Snyder," said Emily, seating herself cozily at the table, settling in for conversation. "I'm awfully glad you've come for the afternoon, Carolina. We can protect each other. I'm a shade uneasy, aren't you?"

"Not really."

"All the better. You can hold my hand if I get scared."

Chris could have hugged Emily.

"Could Deb Snyder identify the man who attacked her?" asked Emily.

"No useful description. Average height, average build."

"It must be the same person who killed Tiffany Sims. I can't imagine there'd be two maniacs suddenly descending on Windom."

"Unless it's a copy-cat attacker," said Carolina, helping herself to another half sandwich.

"That's certainly an idea to consider," said Emily admiringly.

Carolina looked pleased.

"You know that young fellow who was working for Allison Moffitt at Crooked House after she hurt her wrist? Well, Bert went down for gas yesterday morning, and he saw him with Mrs. Moffitt and one of her friends in the Mercedes at the Shell station. He said Mrs. Moffitt barely spoke to him, then just went roaring off."

"Does Bert know this young man's name?"

"Tommy. Tommy Weed, he said it was. Bert told Mrs. Moffitt it probably wasn't a good idea to hire a drifter but, you know, she doesn't listen to anybody, he says. Sort of a law unto herself, according to Bert."

"What does this Tommy Weed look like?"

"Slender, Bert says." Emily would remember that. "Ordinary looking. Not attractive at all. Maybe mid-twenties, though he has trouble judging age any more. Everybody under thirty looks about eighteen to him."

"I believe I've seen him." Chris remembered a young man walking away from the Shell station one day after the bus came in. He'd carried an expensive gym bag. "Where's he staying?"

"I don't know that. Maybe the youth hostel. But they can only stay two nights there, I believe, and he's been here ten days, maybe two weeks."

"Thanks for lunch, Emily. I've got to go." She kissed Carolina on the top of the head. "I'll pick you up about five-thirty."

"Bye, Mom." Apparently Carolina had concluded that sustained sulking was enormously boring.

When Chris got back to her office she requested a check on one Tommy Weed from the state information network, then sent Lep out with a description of Tommy to inquire at the youth hostel and the motels. He had to be staying somewhere.

Now there was the matter of Allison Moffitt. Mrs. Moffitt had said she hadn't been out all day yesterday, yet Bert had seen her at the Shell station with Tommy Weed, who matched the description of the man Tiffany Sims had been drinking with at the Seafarer the night she died.

Chris freshened her lipstick and set out once again for Crooked House.

Chapter 12

CHRIS RANG THE bell at Crooked House and, waiting, turned to look up at the sky. It was a brilliant blue and she wondered if this were what poets called halcyon. She'd never used that word, halcyon. She wasn't even sure how it was pronounced. Halcyon sky, backdrop for the tall firs which rose from neighboring yards.

She was daydreaming. She should be looking for clues. The thing was, she didn't have the faintest idea how to look for clues. The only tools she could rely on for this work were her mind and her intuition, both enhanced by some training and a little experience. Right now, she was aware only that it was taking Mrs. Moffitt a very long time to answer the door. She rang the bell once more.

Now she could hear movement inside, but it was several minutes more before Allison opened the door, and when she did she appeared highly flustered.

"I'm sorry to disturb you again, Mrs. Moffitt. May I come in?"

Allison hesitated, then admitted Chris. "Sorry it took me so long to answer the bell. I was—er, I don't always hear it right away, you see."

There was no one else in the room. The house was silent. Allison nervously indicated a chair for Chris.

"Mrs. Moffitt, is everything all right?"

"Why, certainly." Then, as if to prove it, Allison turned gracious hostess. "Sit down, please. Would you like some coffee? Tea, perhaps?"

"No, thank you." Chris sat down and watched Allison

Moffitt rest herself tentatively on the sofa, a bird in the company of a cat. "Mrs. Moffitt, I'm concerned. Mr. Bertram mentioned that he'd seen you at the service station about ten-thirty Wednesday morning with a young man named Tommy Weed."

"I'm afraid that Mr. Bertram is quite mistaken."

"You weren't at the Shell station yesterday morning then?"

"Oh, yes. Yes, I was. With my housemates, Mrs. Browne and Mrs. Strawbridge. Obviously Mr. Bertram mistook one of them for a young man."

"Who was driving, then?"

"Mrs. Strawbridge," said Allison, then leaned forward. "I'm afraid her license has expired. Some years ago, in fact. But I—well, I still was experiencing some difficulty with my sprained wrist. I'd thought it might be better for Plum to drive, you see. Mr. Bertram is likely accustomed lately to seeing the young man driving and just assumed it was he."

"Where were you going, if I may ask?"

"Portland."

Chris looked surprised. "With your friend who was unaccustomed to driving?"

"It was a foolish idea," conceded Allison. She smiled pleasantly.

"You changed your plans."

"Yes."

"Why is that?"

Allison took a surprising tactic. "Do I need an attorney present? Is this an interrogation?"

"No, you are not obligated to answer my questions, Mrs. Moffitt. I'm here out of concern for you, not to make charges."

Allison was silent. Then, "We decided not to go to Portland when we found the road was washed out. I'm very cautious. I don't like to be subjected to unnecessary hazards."

Chris looked at Allison, trying to gauge this curious

statement. A relatively safe detour caused her to turn back, but she'd been willing to risk an eighty mile trip to the city with an elderly, unpracticed driver behind the wheel?

Her silence goaded the older woman into speech. She said loudly, "That young man, Tommy Weed, was here, but he's gone now. He'd been doing some work for me but decided to leave. He said—he said there had been an accident of some kind, that he was afraid he'd be blamed for it so he—he left."

"When was this?"

"Wednesday morning. Very early. Six or so when he left."

"How did he leave?"

"He left here on foot. Perhaps he intended to hitchhike or to take a bus. I really don't know."

"What sort of accident was he involved in?"

"I'm not sure exactly. Some sort of—of altercation, I believe. He didn't tell us any details." Allison's hands were clammy from the strain of prevarication; she rubbed them together nervously.

"He had a fight with someone?"

"Perhaps so, yes."

"This was Tuesday night?"

Allison nodded.

"What time?"

"I really don't know."

Chris noted again that puzzling vagueness. She persisted. "He came here after the fight? Why would he do that?"

"Yes, he did come here. You see, it was his last day of work for us and we'd paid him off and it seemed he had no place to stay—"

"Where had he been staying before that?"

"I don't know," said Allison truthfully. "I never asked."

"You paid him his wages and—?"

"Yes, and since he had no place to sleep that night, we offered to let him stay here."

"Wasn't that a risk for you? Three elderly women alone in

a house with a young man you really didn't know very much about?"

"Oh, yes, I suppose it was foolhardy. But we'd asked him to stay to dinner, you see, and there was that storm predicted. We did know him, after all. That is, somewhat—well, anyway, being a young person, he naturally decided to go out for a while in the evening. That's understandable. We all went to bed, and then the next morning he said there had been some trouble and he needed to get away for fear of being involved."

The two women looked at each other. There were puzzling aspects to Allison's lacy fabrication, and Chris knew she was not getting accurate information. People stretched the truth for reasons of embarrassment, shame, and ego protection, as well as willfully to mislead. She did not know why Allison Moffitt was lying.

"Where are your housemates, Mrs. Moffitt?"

"Oh. Well, Jane is out, I believe, walking on the beach. And Plum is napping. She hasn't felt well today."

Chris didn't know what else to do. Allison Moffitt's behavior was alternately edgy, arrogant, and cooperative. Since she'd met her only once before and had only Bert to rely on for earlier descriptions, she had no way of knowing if this were ordinary behavior.

"Can you tell me anything about Tommy Weed, Mrs. Moffitt?"

"I really know nothing about him, I'm afraid. Our conversations were quite impersonal and restricted to instructions about his work. He was a fairly good worker, though not one to take much initiative. He was very partial to caring for my car and liked to drive it when I was incapacitated. That's why I hired him, you know. I'd injured my wrist and couldn't drive, so I hired Tommy Weed."

"How did you happen to select him?"

"Oh, I injured my wrist when I took a little fall on the beach. So careless. The paramedic came to offer assistance but I didn't want a fuss made, didn't want to go off in the ambulance. Tommy was on the beach, as it happened, and he offered to walk with me up here to the house. He came around the next day to see if I was all right and asked if I needed any help, said he could do yard work or drive us around to do the errands. It seemed a good idea, and we did need help."

"You didn't check his references or ask around to see if anybody knew him?"

"Actually, I thought he was a local boy when I hired him. I did mention him to Mr. Bertram later and discovered that he wasn't local, but by then he was working out well and I knew it was only temporary so I let him stay on. Perhaps that was foolish."

Chris got up to go. "Mrs. Moffitt, I may stop by in the next day or so to see if you've remembered anything more. And if there is anything you think of, you will call me, won't you?"

"Yes, I will," promised Allison. "Oh, careful of the marble table there, it's rather in the way. You wouldn't want to—to fall and hit your head on it."

"Yes, I see it."

Allison closed the door on Chris Kirksey and leaned against it until she heard the police car drive away. Unsteadily, she walked into Plum's bedroom.

Plum and Jane sat in chairs, their faces chalky with fear. Tommy stood behind them, grinning broadly and slapping the knife against his palm.

"Nice going, Allison baby. I was watching you—thought for a minute there I might be forced to do a little carving, but you came through great."

Allison, having made sure that her friends were all right, turned on her heel without a word to him and went to her bedroom. She slammed the door with a satisfying bang, fell onto her bed and began, at last, to cry.

She could not keep this up much longer. She was old and tired. It was so terrible to feel weak, to be no match for one scrawny, ugly young man. She was certain that Chris Kirksey didn't believe she was telling the truth, but Allison had dared not risk doing more than sending covert mixed messages. And the reference to the marble table—how could that possibly carry any meaning at all to anyone who had not seen Tiffany Sims sprawled beside it?

She squeezed her eyes shut in despair, trying to blot out the look she'd seen on Tommy's face, the triumphant gloating of a despicable and unfeeling young man who would kill them all if he felt he had to. And there was not one thing that Allison could think of to prevent it. They might just as well be chained in their rooms, but the awful part was that Tommy didn't even have to do that to control them. Like some purse-snatching thug on the street, he had only to take what he wanted from the weak and the vulnerable, who fearfully surrendered to the demands of his strength.

He was the predator.

They were his prey.

Chapter 13

AFTER CHRIS KIRKSEY'S second visit to Crooked House, Tommy sent the old ladies to their rooms and got busy. An hour later he assembled the troops. That's what he called them, "the troops," and his tone was mocking. Small wonder, for he commanded, through self-appropriated power, an elderly and rebellious trio of reluctant followers. Even his lieutenant, if that's what Allison was, would like to lead a mutiny at the first opportunity—if she had the strength, which she clearly did not.

There was, Allison saw at once, a change in Tommy, a new excited kind of energy, as if Chris's visit that afternoon had raised the stakes in his crazy warfare.

He had a new weapon which he proudly showed them.

On the kitchen table sat a wine bottle filled with gasoline he'd siphoned from the Mercedes. He had fashioned a wick from a strip of dish towel and had built a crude, but as far as Allison could determine, effective bomb.

"I figure a butcher knife has its uses, but it's a little slow," he explained. "I like this better. Now I got me two deterrents."

His troops regarded him in silent loathing.

"The thing is that I'm going to have to send you, Allison baby, out on an errand, and you might start getting the idea that one man with one knife at the throat of a hostage is worth a gamble. But with this little dude—" He thumped the side of the squat jug proudly. "With this, I could take two people and this whole house up with just a flick of a match."

"That's very clever, Mr. Weed, but I am wondering if it

114

wouldn't be better for you to put your energy into leaving here rather than in continuing to keep us captive."

"Oh, no. You fixed that, telling that stupid woman cop I was gone. They'll be looking for me now on the road."

"You could disguise yourself." This was Plum's suggestion.

Tommy ignored it. "All in good time, I'll leave. Where I *know* they aren't looking for me now is right here. In a few days, I'll make my move."

"A few days! Oh, dear," said Plum, "I don't know if I can stand having you here for a few days more."

"You'll stand it."

Plum shook her head decisively. "I don't mean to be rude, Tommy, but you are a *very* difficult person to have around."

Allison was aware that she and her friends had thus far stood firmly together without parceling out blame or recriminations. Their concern for one another's welfare and for mutual protection against a common adversary seemed further to cement their solid relationship. But she also saw that cracks were beginning to appear.

The strain was most evident in Plum, whose confinement in the house had been the longest. She had not been out since the night they'd dragged Tiffany's body down to the beach. She liked to potter around in the yard amongst the geraniums she'd so cheerfully planted in pots and placed on the deck and in strategically sheltered spots in the yard. She'd commenced building a little rock garden, nestling sweet alyssum and Scottish moss into crevices between stones and big rocks laboriously brought up from the beach. And her kitchen garden of herbs required her attention, the parsley and basil to be gathered and dried. Not allowed to tend the green growing things she loved, Plum began to resent her confinement even more. She was also feeling the weary responsibility for all the meals.

"My geraniums need clipping," she fretted. "Just look at

those dead heads on them. It's disgraceful. And the alyssum is going to seed. It won't bloom again if it isn't cut back."

"I cannot believe you are complaining about such inconsequential matters as those flowers," said Jane sharply. "We're trying to survive here and you're nattering about flowers? You can buy new flowers if they all go to seed. That is, you can if we manage to live through this incarceration. We're being held hostage, for God's sake!"

"And whose fault is that, I'd like to know. It seems to me that *one* of us is pretty much responsible for this whole dreary business."

"That statement is beneath you, Plum. It is unforgivable." And Jane took her unforgiveness into her room and slammed the door. She was shaking with fury. Jane avoided personal confrontation, limiting her disagreements with others to larger political, artistic, and social issues. In all their lengthy friendship, she could honestly say that she and Plum had never exchanged angry words. She would not have been surprised—indeed she half expected it—to have been attacked so unkindly for their present plight by Allison. But by Plum? Gentle, accepting Plum? It was like being bitten by a rabid butterfly.

It seemed to Jane now that there was a facet of Plum's personality that had long been dormant. Under pressure, Plum was behaving badly, letting out a stream of whining complaints. And if there was anything Jane detested, it was a whiner.

Plum, believing herself maligned and deliberately misunderstood, resorted to guerrilla warfare in the kitchen. When they gathered for their afternoon tea at the kitchen table, she mentioned the meatloaf she was preparing for their supper.

"And what am I to eat?" asked Jane.

Plum executed a snippy, indifferent shrug.

"You're just being spiteful!" Jane accused.

"I do the best I can." Plum set her chin stubbornly, but it quivered.

"You could at least cook more vegetables."

"Cook them yourself."

"I will!"

"Not in my kitchen, you won't. Besides there aren't any." Plum was triumphant.

"Shut up, both of you." For once Allison was in agreement with Tommy's crude order.

"I can't stand this!" wailed Plum and tearfully left the table.

"Please excuse me. I'm going to my room." Jane departed also with an ostentatious display of dignity.

Tommy tipped himself back in his chair and tapped the butcher knife against his knee. He turned his yellow eyes on Allison, who sat quietly with her hands folded in her lap.

"Well, Allison baby, it's your turn to go running off crying like Lady Plum and plain Jane."

"Mr. Weed, we are all exhausted."

"I'm not. Don't you believe for a minute that I'm tired out."

Allison, who rarely quibbled when she knew she was right, forged ahead. "I think it would be easier on all of us if we could have a little time for exercise and fresh air. Plum especially needs to get outdoors. It isn't that those flowers are important in themselves. They aren't. But she sees their neglect and feels like a prisoner—"

"She *is* a prisoner, lady. My prisoner. What do you think I'm doing here, running a rest home for raisins because I got nothing else to do?"

"I'm aware, of course, that we are your hostages, Mr. Weed. The neighbors will also be aware that something is wrong if they don't see us behaving normally. They all know that Plum takes pride in her garden. What will they think if they see it neglected? They might begin to wonder, they'll start coming over to see if we're all right." This was not exactly accurate. The houses immediately surrounding Crooked House belonged to absent owners with whom the

women had had virtually no contact. Tommy didn't have to
know that, however.

"So what do you want?"

"I want you to let us resume some of our normal
activities."

"No."

"Why not?"

"Because I say so."

"I see."

A slow smile spread over Tommy's unattractive face. He'd
won.

Allison rose to clear the tea things off the table, quickly
turning away so that her small victory would not be betrayed
to him. Tommy liked the power he held over them, even in
inconsequential matters. She'd guessed he would deny her
request, and that once denied, he wouldn't hold it up for
review. There was a small chance that someone might notice
Plum's neglected garden, slightly more chance that shop-
keepers might notice their absence in the village. It did occur
to Allison that what was far more likely to be noticed was
that the women failed to pick up their mail each day at the
post office. It was a small hope, but it was all she had at the
moment.

Boredom was not a natural state for Allison, who believed
that people with inner resources had no reason to be bored.
And if one were blessed with both inner and financial
resources, as was she, it was singularly lacking in gratitude to
wallow in boredom.

But the tedium of being held captive by Tommy Weed
was wearing her down. Allison *was* bored. She found it
difficult to concentrate, even on music and literature, which
had been the foundations of lifelong pleasure. And her
quick, active mind was dulled by constantly turning over and
rejecting plans to end Tommy's hold over them. She knew
now what the phrase "at wit's end" truly meant.

She was tired of feeling weak and trapped, tired of
circuitous battles with Tommy, whose inferior intelligence

was balanced by his superior strength. She felt a blind fury toward him—he was ignorant, uncouth, unattractive, and quite probably crazy. Unlike Plum, she could not find it within herself to feel sorry for him, even to try to understand the social and biological disadvantages that had produced such a miserable human being. Even the initial kindness she'd thought he possessed she now saw as a calculated way of ingratiating himself to her. She conceded that she'd been a wrong-headed old fool to have allowed herself to be so easily taken in by him. That acknowledgment only depressed her.

It further depressed her to acknowledge that her own stubbornness was responsible for the ease with which Tommy had been able to imprison them. Those fixed storm windows in the bedrooms, that she'd insisted upon to keep intruders out, now contributed to their captivity. And she'd had to have the mirrored glass in all the windows—oh, she'd been very definite about that, she thought bitterly. Didn't want nosy people peering in at them. Well, she'd got what she wanted: no passerby could see in, could see a frantic rescue signal. But she could see out, could look to her heart's content at freedom beyond her grasp.

They were all coming unstrung, Allison could see that. They had the remainder of the afternoon to be got through, and then the long evening when Tommy would turn on some abominable sports program and force them to sit there watching with him like some bizarre family of morons.

They had reassembled in the living room after the disastrous attempt at normalcy during tea. Tommy sat slapping the carving knife against his palm and staring into space. Plum sat squarely in the center of the sofa, her mouth tight with anger, her hands busily spinning off crocheted squares. Now and then she would furiously unravel some yarn, as though her stitchery had tightened with the anger from her mouth. Jane was still in her room. She and Plum were not speaking.

Would they sit like this till evening, Allison wondered.

And then, through tomorrow and all the tomorrows which would make up their lives until Tommy decreed it was safe to leave? And then undoubtedly he would haul one or more of them into the car for some hellish and interminable ride to California or Washington where—assuming they weren't all killed in some tire-screeching freeway chase with the police—he would feel obliged to blow them all up with that homemade bomb of his so that they couldn't testify against him. How on earth did she, Allison Moffitt, ever become embroiled in such a plot?

Plum put aside her needlework, got up out of her chair, and went into the kitchen.

Tommy watched her go, watched her putter in the kitchen and then, amazed, saw her open the back door. He was on his feet and into the kitchen like an arrow.

"What the hell do you think you're doing?"

"Why, I'm going to feed that cat. I heard him mewing at the back door. He's hungry."

"No!"

"No?"

"I told you *no*—are you hard of hearing?"

"Why, yes, but only so slightly. I *did* hear the cat. He wants feeding."

"You'll not feed that goddamned cat. Let him go hungry."

"Tommy, you're downright cruel."

"You got it, lady. What I say goes in this house."

Plum marched herself back into the living room and resumed her place on the sofa where she burst into tears. "That cat never did anything to you, Tommy Weed. I do *not* understand how you can behave so wickedly, I truly do not."

Allison watched in dismay as her friend sniffled into her hanky. She fervently wished Plum would not allow Tommy to see signs of weakness. It only made things worse. Tommy was a tyrant, and he thrived on the weakness of others.

Chapter 14

CON SNYDER MARCHED into the village police station. He wanted to see some action.

"So, have you found that degenerate who attacked my daughter?" He knew the answer perfectly well, knew that Chris would have informed him immediately of an arrest, knew that even if she'd failed to do so, the humming village grapevine would have carried the news within moments of any official action.

"No, Con. The closest we have to a suspect is an itinerant named Tommy Weed who was in Windom for a week or so." Chris picked up the print-out report from the state information network. "Tommy Weed. Age twenty-five. Lengthy juvenile record. Some petty stuff as an adult— disorderly conduct, DUI, assault, shoplifting, resisting arrest. Not a model citizen, but not a candidate for the Ten Most Wanted list either."

Conrad harrumphed. "Probably done a lot of stuff he didn't get caught at."

"Probably." Chris often found agreement disarming. Especially with Conrad Snyder who loved to be right.

"And this degenerate was right here in Windom, running free, and you just let him hang around until he attacked some innocent girls?"

"I knew he was here, yes. This is a free country, Con. We don't throw people in jail because they're unattractive or unemployed."

Con thought this was too bad. "Coddling, that's what we do. We're so busy coddling criminals, it's the ordinary citizen

121

who is in peril of his life. That's what wrong with this society. All you bleeding-heart liberals—"

"How is Deb?"

Conrad was torn between a desire to castigate a favorite foe and to talk about his daughter. Family ties won.

"She's made of the right stuff." Con frequently sounded like thirty-second TV spot announcements. "She's coping." Just in case Chris might take this as a signal to let up on her investigation, he added, "It's not easy on her. Or on her mother."

"Or on you."

He brushed this aside; being weak was women's work. "I manage." He set his jaw and clenched his fists. Macho man.

"I'd like to talk to Deb again when she's up to it."

"Why?" His eyes narrowed suspiciously. Father protector.

"She may have remembered something. Besides, in a situation like this, it's often helpful to talk about the traumatic incident as much as possible. Repetition makes it more real and that reality makes it less frightening."

"You sound like one of those half-baked psychologists."

"Well, there are certainly plenty of those around. That doesn't diminish the value of understanding human behavior, however. What seems true to me, Con, is that we both want Deb to heal and get on with her life."

"What I want is for that bastard to be caught, and that's your job."

"Yes, it is."

"Your job's on the line, missy!"

"My job and the way I do it is always on the line." They exchanged level looks. "When would be a good time for me to talk with Deb?"

"I don't know. Now, I guess. Call Gloria."

Deb appeared in better spirits than when Chris had last seen her. She sat in the Snyder family room surrounded by a coterie of teenaged girl friends, all bouncing between sincere solicitude and ghoulish hunger to share some limelight with the star. Deb gave a world-weary sigh when Chris asked to speak to her privately. She led the way into her bedroom and flopped down on her bed, curling her knees up into a fetal position and supporting her head with the heel of one hand while the other picked nervously at the nap on the bedspread.

"So what do you want to know?"

"I'd like to know how you're feeling today."

"Fine."

Such an all-purpose, masking word. Fine. I was attacked last night by a maniac and I feel fine. I got a D on an exam and I feel fine. I'm unemployed, unloved, overworked, terminally ill, newly divorced—and I'm fine.

"I'm glad you're feeling better, Deb. I'd like you to go over your account of the incident once more."

"What for? I already told you."

"I know. Sometimes in the re-telling you remember things. And usually talking about something unpleasant like this helps us to get over it faster."

Deb gave a persecuted sigh and recounted the incident without significant variation from the first version.

"It would be helpful to the investigation if we went down on the beach so that you could show me exactly where the attack occurred."

"Don't you believe me?" Deb stopped picking at the bedspread nap and gave Chris a petulant look.

"Is there any reason why I shouldn't believe you?" asked Chris mildly.

"No."

Deb, having informed her mother and goggle-eyed friends that she must visit the "scene of the crime," trailed after Chris to the waiting patrol car. Joan of Arc off to burn at the stake.

The tide was in, and Deb claimed that this was the cause of her confusion. Besides, it had been dark last night. No, she couldn't account for the absence of driftwood where she'd been dragged, she just knew that's what had happened.

Maybe they'd been nearer to the Seafarer than she'd thought. She was confused, she couldn't remember. Why couldn't Chris just leave her alone?

Chris well understood that people, particularly witnesses and suspects, were far too complex to judge solely on body language. Some avoided eye contact out of shame or embarrassment or chagrin, while others looked her square in the eye and boldly lied; they changed or embroidered their stories, forgot crucial details or were sincerely mistaken. She trusted her intuition when the words she heard and the behavior she observed and the facts she gathered did not fit together. And more often than not, this intuitive skepticism led her to dig deeper for the truth. Presently she struggled to construct a pattern to fit together logically what she'd heard from Allison Moffitt and Deb Snyder. She closed her eyes and reviewed Deb's performance.

Performance.

That was it.

Chris had the feeling that Deb was giving a performance. Here was a youngster who had dramatically fled a friend's house, alone and at night, to walk on the same stretch of beach where another young woman had been murdered. Deb had been attacked, commanding the attention of friends, family, and police. She was being rapidly elevated to superstar status in the village. And she was reveling in the role.

Allison Moffitt was a different matter altogether. There was about this woman a strong sense of straightforwardness. She did not waste time playing games or hiding behind a mask. If what Bert had said about her was to be believed, she was opinionated, eccentric, and shrewd. Why then was Chris picking up such strong signals of caution, evasion, and a wholly inappropriate willingness to present herself as vague and stumbling?

Performance.

Chris said the word out loud. Both Deb Snyder and Allison Moffitt were giving performances. But why?

A tapping on the door interrupted her thoughts. "Come in."

Chris had left word with Emily to have Bert call or stop by the office. Bert was not completely comfortable with telephones, so it was no surprise to Chris when the contractor ambled into her office, swept off the fishing hat he liked to wear, and eased himself into a chair by her desk.

"What do you need?"

"Information."

He nodded. Bert saw no reason to clutter up the air with unnecessary words.

"How many bedrooms are there at Crooked House, Bert?"

"Three." He grinned. "And you oughta see them, especially Mrs. Moffitt's. I got a tour of the house after the ladies all moved in." Let there be no misunderstanding about how Bert came to know what Allison Moffitt's boudoir looked like.

"There's no guest room?"

He shook his head emphatically. "She wanted three big bedrooms and that's what she got. Said any overnight visitors could stay in a motel."

Allison Moffitt's prim living room was decidedly not the sort where a visitor might toss a sleeping bag on the floor. Chris thought of the beautiful antique furniture. Those marble top tables. She frowned. Where had Tommy Weed slept on Tuesday night?

"Another subject then, Bert. Mrs. Moffitt says you must have been mistaken when you said you saw her at the Shell station Wednesday morning with Tommy Weed. She said it was her housemate, Mrs. Strawbridge, who was driving, not Tommy Weed."

Bert considered this, leaning forward, brow wrinkled in recollection of the scene. "Well, Chris, I admit I need my glasses to look up a number in the phone book, but I can sure tell an old lady from a young guy behind the wheel of a car."

"She says you're mistaken."

"Well, I say I'm not. Tommy Weed was driving that car. That lady named Plum wasn't even in it. Mrs. Moffitt was in the passenger seat and that other lady, Mrs. Browne, was in back. Check with Woody's son at the Shell station, though I don't think that kid pays a whole lot of attention to what's going on around him half the time." Bert looked perplexed. "I could be mistaken, but I'm ninety-eight per cent sure I'm not. Why would Mrs. Moffitt tell a tale about that?"

"I don't know."

After Bert left, Chris pondered that question. Say that the women had foolishly offered to let Tommy Weed stay with them on Tuesday night. Never mind where—pitch a sleeping bag in the yard or on the deck. And he goes out in the evening for a beer at the Seafarer, meets Tiffany, and they leave together. Neither had a car. Would he be allowed to take the Mercedes? Not likely. So they walk on the beach, he gets amorous, she resists, they struggle. She either falls or he strikes her, the blow is fatal. He panics and throws her in the sea, goes back to Crooked House. The next morning he tells the women there's been an accident. Why on earth would the women help him get out of town? Because he threatens them, of course. He's young and strong, they're old and vulnerable. They agree to drive him to Portland or maybe just up the road far enough so that he can hitch a ride, whatever. That might explain Mrs. Moffitt's behavior. They'd been coerced into giving him assistance and were now frightened of the repercussions.

Tommy Weed was gone.

So who attacked Deb Snyder?

If she'd made up the story, then they needed to look elsewhere for Tommy Weed.

If Tommy Weed had attacked Deb Snyder, he was still in Windom. But where?

"I turned up nothing but zeroes at the motels." Lep lounged in a side chair in Chris's office. She had finally trained him not to put his feet on her desk, though she'd been less successful in discouraging his insolent glances. She noted the disrespect inherent in his posture.

"You turned up zeroes?" Somehow Lep and zeroes seemed to fit together.

"Yeah, he didn't register in any motel in town."

"And the youth hostel?"

"They think he was there one night, week or so ago. They can't be sure. You know how those freaks are, don't pay attention too good. They get ten dozen guys a month there matching his description anyway."

"Anybody at the state park remember a lone camper on foot?"

"Nope." Lep looked I-told-you-so pleased with his negative report. Chris had a strong urge to smack him across his impudent mouth, hard. "So, what's next?"

"What would you do next?"

The question startled him. He was good at puncturing other people's balloons, not in sending them aloft himself. He appeared, from the pained expression on his face, to be engaged in cogitation.

"Well—" His face brightened at having hatched an idea. "I say we just sit tight and wait for the next development."

By Friday, Jane and Plum were behaving like a pair of sullen teenagers, sticking their noses into the air in an elaborate display of disregard for one another's existence and sustaining such long icy silences that it was clear that something had to be done.

Peacemaking was hardly Allison's forte, her accustomed role being that of combatant. Her approach was direct, her choice of words dismal.

"The only way we are going to survive is for the two of you to stop this adolescent bickering. I want you to make up with one another and to do it now."

Plum and Jane promptly regressed from adolecents to kindergarteners.

"She started it."

"I did no such thing."

"You most certainly did."

"I most certainly did *not!*"

"Please! Both of you!"

Two pairs of hostile eyes turned on the peacemaker.

"You always think you know what's best for everybody, Allison. Always ordering us around—you're just plain *bossy!*"

"She's right. You always want to have your own way."

"Well, of course, I do." Allison was genuinely puzzled. Didn't everybody want her own way? Wasn't this a profound truth of human nature?

Tommy had brightened at this blossoming conflict among the women and grinned as the charges flew, first from Plum, then from Jane.

"And *you* get to go out while *I* never even get to step out the door to water my dying geraniums."

"If you hadn't been so arrogantly certain that you're a fine judge of people, you'd never have brought Tommy Weed here to work."

Stung, Allison struck back, seizing a cannon when a fly-swatter would have done the job. "And if you hadn't killed your husband, Tommy wouldn't have had any reason to come here in the first place." Appalled at what she'd said, Allison apologized at once and with rare humility. "I am truly, truly sorry, Jane."

"And so you should be."

Plum burst into tears.

Tommy looked disappointed. The fight was over.

Before lunch, Tommy dispatched Allison to the grocery store.

He could not resist his repetitious litany of threats should she reveal his presence in the house. "You go straight to the store and get this stuff and you come straight back here. You understand?"

"Yes."

"And you get me some beer. Two cases. And some Twinkies and some of them Pattie Pies, the ones with cherry filling."

"It's all on the list."

Allison was at the back door with her hand on the knob when Jane called, "Pick up the mail, please. And take these letters to mail for me."

Allison's heart sank. She'd hoped that failure to pick up their mail would serve as an alarm.

"Oh, no. You don't send any mail out of here till I've read it," said Tommy.

"That's censorship! You will *not* read my mail!" Jane was ever vigilant concerning the abrogation of civil rights.

Tommy, who had systematically restricted the women's civil rights for nearly a week, was unmoved. "Then you won't send it out. Get going, Allison baby. You've got twenty minutes."

"That's not nearly enough time," Allison objected.

"Twenty minutes!" Tommy put his face unpleasantly close to hers. "I'm locking these two in the bathroom as soon as you leave and I'm gonna time you. And if you're not standing right here in twenty minutes, you know what I intend to do? I intend to blow up the damned house—with them in it." He patted the wine jug filled with gasoline. "Twenty minutes, lady. And remember my buddy here, in case you feel like shooting off your mouth." He leered, gesturing an explosion. *"Ka-boooom!"*

The clock in the Mercedes read 10:14 as Allison backed out of the garage. Her hands trembled with fright and fury.

At the Gullway Market Allison flitted about like a butterfly gone berserk, selecting items from the flowery-scripted list Plum had provided. Indiscriminately, she filled plastic bags of produce—limp lettuce, bruised pears, what did it matter? It seemed to take so long just to find things. Plum usually did the marketing, and the layout of the little store was unfamiliar to Allison.

The clock over the deli section read 10:21. Thirteen minutes left. She'd never make it home in time.

She grabbed the beer for Tommy, ignoring the Henry Weinhard in favor of two cases of plain generic-brand, a small but satisfying passive-aggressive act. She threw into the cart a dozen packages each of Twinkies and Pattie Pies, some cheese and a chunk of fatty bologna. With this diet, Tommy might eventually die of clogged arteries, but Allison didn't think she could wait that long to be rid of him. This thought made a giggle rise in her throat, and she fought a wave of hysteria.

She paused to wipe her forehead with a tissue, leaning heavily against the grocery cart, trying to think. Why didn't she just scream out, right here in the middle of the store, that Tommy Weed was holding them hostage, threatening to kill her friends?

Because, she answered herself, because in real life people did not react the way they did in the movies, leaping into decisive action, rushing off to corner the villain. If she were to blurt out the truth, these nice normal shoppers would look at her in bewilderment and ask, "You're being held *what?* Repeat that, lady—you say somebody is going to blow up your house if you're not back from the store in twenty minutes?" They'd exchange alarmed glances, suggest that she sit down a minute and and rest, maybe have a nice drink of water. Precious time would tick by while they evaluated her story and her sanity, and then it would be too late.

It was now 10:26. Allison closed her eyes as if that very gesture would stop the hands on the clock.

She had an idea. If she could not risk asking for help outright, she could leave a note here. "Held hostage at Crooked House. Send help!" Even if it were regarded as a prank, someone surely would check it out, given the murder in the village. Yes, a note. That would give her time to get home, would get Plum and Jane out of immediate danger, and they could all be prepared for help when it came.

Hastily, Allison wrote the note on the back of Plum's

grocery list, then pushed her cart to the checkout stand where a small cheerful-looking woman and a pretty teenaged girl chatted leisurely with the storekeeper.

"I don't know what'll happen next, Emily, I swear I don't," said Orin Brixby sadly.

Allison rattled her shopping cart in agitation, signaling her impatience.

Orin marched to his own drummer. Languorously, he placed Emily Bertram's purchases into a sack, rearranging them for a more compact fit, never missing a beat of his soliloquy. "First that Sims girl, and now Deb Snyder. Let me tell you, if I had a daughter I'd keep a close eye on her. Your mother's got the right idea, Carolina, having you stay at Emily's. Just can't be too careful, I say."

Allison rattled her cart again.

Orin nodded to her pleasantly. "Oh, hello, Mrs. Moffitt. Heard about our excitement?"

"No, Mr. Brixby, I'm afraid I'm in a hur—"

"Con Snyder's daughter was attacked there on the beach in front of your place."

Allison felt a chill. "When was this?"

"Wednesday night, about eleven. Awful, that's what it is." Orin shook his head. "You okay, Mrs. Moffitt?"

"Yes, thank you." Allison had visibly paled. "I—I'm just in a hurry, Mr. Brixby."

"Oh, sure," said Orin, concluding his transaction with Emily. He then turned smartly to Allison's cart and, like a brisk little robot, bent and straightened as he removed each item and chanted out the price. As he was counting out Allison's change, the phone rang.

"Just a minute there, Mrs. Moffitt," he said, "and I'll carry your things to the car for you."

"Never mind, Orin," said Emily Bertram, "Carolina and I are going your way, Mrs. Moffitt. Let us help you."

Allison, wild to leave the place, didn't care who assisted her. Hurriedly, she tucked the rescue note under a flimsy cardboard display of peppermint candies, hoped for the best, and followed Emily and Carolina out the door.

It was 10:31. She had three minutes to get home.

"Bert has spoken of you often, Mrs. Moffitt," said Emily, chattily. "He certainly enjoyed doing the remodeling of your house."

Allison nodded distractedly, unlocked the Mercedes's trunk, opened it wide, and gazed down at the three telephones that Tommy had removed from the bedrooms at Crooked House.

Emily and Carolina gaped at the unexpected contents of the trunk, while Allison, with great aplomb, thanked them, spryly leaped into the Mercedes, and drove off. It didn't matter if they regarded her as weird and rude. Nothing mattered except getting home.

It was 10:37.

She'd been gone twenty-three minutes.

Tommy sat at the kitchen table, grinning. "You're late."

"Where are Plum and Jane?" Allison slumped against the door frame, panting and trembling.

Without removing his amused gaze from her face, Tommy called out, "Come on out here, old biddies."

Plum and Jane, looking like chastised children, crept into the kitchen. Allison expelled a huge sigh of relief. She understood the truth: Tommy, with his innate shrewdness about human nature, had been certain that Allison wouldn't dare ask help from people whose first inclination would be to disbelieve her story. That's why he'd given her an impossible time frame, to put pressure on her, to keep her focused on the clock.

Winnie Ruth Brixby took over the cash register at the Gullway Market while Orin trotted off to restock the canned soup shelf. Winnie Ruth, obsessively tidy by nature, clucked in annoyance at the sight of a piece of paper tucked under the peppermint candy display. People were always leaving grocery lists on the counter, cluttering it up, making a mess.

Why couldn't people throw away their own trash instead of leaving it for others to dispose of? Winnie Ruth snatched up the offending paper and wadded it into a tight ball, then, bristling with self-rightousness, she tossed Allison's plea for help into the wastebasket.

Chapter 15

THE SMELL OF baking apples and simmering onions came from the kitchen where Plum, apparently mollified by the fresh supply of groceries, bustled about preparing dinner. The spicy and sharp aromas wrapped the house in a coziness that did not touch Allison's heart. It had been five hours since she'd left her note pleading for help at the Gullway Market. No one had come. No one was going to come.

She had set up a card table in front of her wing chair and sat playing solitaire. Or what she remembered as solitaire. She hadn't played in years. She disliked games of all sorts and held a particular distaste for card games. She'd been at this for half an hour when she set the deck down with a sigh of defeat. "I lost again."

"Unlucky at cards, lucky at love. That's you, Allison baby."

"Perhaps you'd like to play, Mr. Weed."

"Naw, I like gin. You play gin?"

"No."

"It figures."

"Actually, I don't care for card games at all. I'd hoped it might help pass the time to play." She gathered up the cards into a neat stack.

"Well, okay, gimme the deck. I'll play." He dragged up a stool and began shuffling the cards. The butcher knife lay across his knees.

Allison watched him lay out the cards. He had square hands with stubby fingers, and his nails were not clean.

Disgusting. He played for a while in silence. The cards fell in his favor, and he smirked at her.

"Won!" he announced gleefully. He set out another game. "So you're bored, are you?"

"I find being held hostage tedious, yes."

"I let you go out today, didn't I?"

"Yes."

He studied the cards he'd dealt himself. "All them busy-bodies in the village talking about me?"

"I don't know."

"Who did you see? Tell me everybody you saw."

He sounds like a child, thought Allison, wanting to know the business of grown-ups. "I saw the Brixbys who own the market," she told him. She thought about the note again with a tug of disappointment.

"Yeah? Who else?"

"Mrs. Bertram and Carolina—"

There was a brief pause and Tommy's hand paused over the card he was picking up. "Who's that? Another old biddy?"

"No, she's a teenaged girl."

"Carolina—oh, yeah." He could see her, striding down the sidewalk, her golden hair bouncing on her back, remembered her self-assured handling of the boys in front of the candy store and how old man Brixby had suddenly materialized in the doorway, like he was prepared to defend somebody important. And indeed Carolina was important. Tommy, who paid keen attention to other people's conversations, had learned that Carolina was the daughter of Windom's police chief. This bit of information he'd re-examined several times; he had a hunch it was going to be useful to him in the near future.

"Do you know Mrs. Bertram?" asked Allison conversationally.

"Naw." Absently, he'd gone through the stack of cards in his hand twice without success.

"Mrs. Bertram said there had been an attack on another young woman."

His head shot up, startled.

"Wednesday night," said Allison, her eyes on his.

He snorted. "And you think I did it?"

"I heard you go out after you locked us in that night." Allison's voice was calm, carefully devoid of accusation.

Tommy licked his lips. "Where was this attack?"

"On the beach. Near this house. I don't know precisely where."

"And you think I did it?"

"I don't know, Mr. Weed."

"They think I did it though, the village idiots? That big-boobed lady cop and now her daughter? She thinks so?"

"I don't know what others think. I expect they believe that one person is responsible for two attacks on women."

"Well, I didn't do it. Yeah, I went outside. I been cooped up here with you weepy women till I'm crazy. Yeah, I went outside, just to stand in the night air and breathe for a while. Yeah, I was out—but not on the beach."

He looked at the cards in his hands as though wondering how they'd come to be there, then threw them down savagely. "Stupid game. Stupid life!" He stood up, nearly overturning the table, the knife in his hand. "I always get accused of things. All my life, I'm being accused. Nobody ever thinks I'm innocent. Never. That Tiffany, I didn't kill her. She came back here with me of her own free will. She was looking for a good time, she wasn't any angel. She knew what I wanted. I was trying to catch her, it was like a game, then she fell and hit her head. She was dead but I didn't kill her. It was an accident!"

He moved away from the table in agitation, then pointed the knife at Allison. "You think life is fair, don't you, Miss Rich Lady? *Fair!* Maybe it is for people like you, but not for people like me. I'm always the one blamed when things go wrong. My mother blamed me for being born, for God's sake. As if I'd asked to be, as if I'd screwed around and created myself like some goddamned amoeba. I always get blamed. It's always my fault. My mother, teachers at school, social workers, all those goddamned people pointing fingers at me and saying it's my own fault. All of 'em out to get me, out to screw me over, out to squeeze the life out of me." He ran out of words and stood pale and shaking.

Allison said, "I'm sorry, Mr. Weed."

"And I don't need none of your goddamned pity slop. Everybody's sorry but nobody ever did anything for me. All I ever got was hassled and hurt. It's me against the world. And you're part of the world, Allison baby. You're out to get me just like all the rest." With a swift, almost graceful motion, he whipped the knife to her throat. "The difference is that this time, I've got the upper hand."

At lunch, Tommy decided the women were trying to poison him.

He did not like dishes in which he could not readily identify all the ingredients and, in any case, he had a woefully underdeveloped palate, suspiciously questioning any food that was new to him. He viewed with alarm the vegetarian casserole Plum had made to please Jane.

"What is this crap?"

"It's a vegetarian casserole, Tommy. Fresh vegetables, parmesan cheese, and little herbs."

"What kind of herbs?"

"Oh, that's my little secret." Plum's tone was playful, designed to cajole suspicious boys to eat what was served.

To Tommy, who was not playful, secrets signaled potential danger. He pushed his plate away. "I can't eat this stuff. You could be poisoning me with it and I wouldn't even know it."

"Why, Tommy, that's downright insulting."

"Yeah, well, I don't want any more of these funny dishes. From now on I want only food that's wrapped or that comes from a can or that I personally see cooked. You hear?"

"Mr. Weed, be reasonable. How could this food be

poisoned? We're all of us eating it. Really!" But Jane could save her logic for someone who could follow it.

"You, Lady Plum, open me up a can of tuna fish."

"You want a nice tuna salad sandwich?"

"No! I want you to bring the can opener and a can of tuna fish to this table and open it, right in front of me. And get me a beer which I will personally open." His eyes never left Plum as she moved glacially about the kitchen to do his bidding. He forked tuna from the can into his mouth, glaring at the women. "I'm no fool. Not me. You won't poison me, old ladies."

It hadn't occurred to Allison to poison the odious Tommy Weed, but now that he'd brought it up, she gazed at him reflectively.

Allison had never seriously considered murdering anyone, deliberately, with premeditation. And she knew that she could not poison Tommy Weed. Oh, she could do murder. She believed anyone could, given the right circumstances. If she ever had to defend herself against Tommy, she knew she'd fight like a demon against him with all her strength. That, of course, was the problem; she was not strong. Furthermore she was unpracticed: she had never, in all her life, fought with another human being. Except with words.

Well, maybe she could talk him to death.

No, she could not poison Tommy. She could, however, make him very sick, render him unconscious or ineffective so that they could escape. She wished she'd thought of it before he had, for now that the idea was in his mind, it would be much harder to carry out.

Harder, but not impossible. She'd give it some thought. Later.

At the moment another crisis was brewing. Plum had scraped the remains of Tommy's unfinished tuna fish into a plastic bowl for the little black cat she'd been feeding. She headed for the back door to set the food on the steps.

"Where the hell do you think you're going?"

Plum opened the door and set the dish down as she spoke. "I'm just feeding the cat, Tommy."

"Get back in here and bring that food with you."

"It's already in the bowl, Tommy." The cat, mewing, tail held high in anticipation, attacked the food instantly.

"Now, Tommy, you said you weren't going to eat anything that wasn't freshly opened. What's the harm in giving the leftover tuna to the cat?"

"Because I said no."

"Well, I'm afraid it's too late. The poor little thing is already eating it. He's so hungry."

"Oh, yeah?" Tommy fingered the knife and, catlike himself, rose from the table, roughly brushed Plum aside at the door and stooped toward the cat.

"Here, kitty, kitty. . ."

"Whatever are you doing, Tommy?"

"I'm teaching you an obedience lesson, Lady Plum." He stretched out his left hand, his right gripping the butcher knife. "Nice kitty, kitty. Come here."

The cat, like Tommy, had been abandoned, mistreated, left to cope with a harsh world of pain and cruelty; like Tommy, the cat was ever alert to danger. As he reached for the animal with destructive intent, the cat struck first. Razor claws raked Tommy's hand and with an angry hiss, the cat vanished around the corner of the house.

"I'll get that son of a bitch yet." Tommy's yellow eyes, not very different from the cat's eyes, smouldered. Plum handed him a paper towel to absorb the ribbons of blood on his hand. He said softly, "The next time you feed that cat, I'll kill him, you hear?"

Allison, who had taken in this scene from the kitchen doorway, turned in disgust.

She thought again of poison.

"I gotta get out of here," thought Tommy. "I can't stand being cooped up with these twittery women any longer. There's gotta be a way for me to get out of here."

The television blared mindlessly, but Tommy wasn't watching it. He was watching the women. Allison and Jane were reading, Plum was crocheting and occasionally glancing up at the TV. He would not allow them to go to bed until he wanted to be rid of them. They had to sit there as long as he told them to.

How could he escape? His original plan of taking one of the old ladies along as hostage had long since lost all appeal. He liked Plum the best but she was too frail, too slow, too sensitive, too weepy. And plain Jane was not to be trusted. Anyway, she gave him the creeps, the way she looked at him as if he were some kind of deviant, which he was not. And Allison with her superior ways and her open dislike—well, he had plans for her, and they didn't include an escape in the Mercedes.

No, he'd not take any of these biddies hostage. It was all he could do to stay with them here in this house.

But a hostage was powerfully protective. He needed somebody who wouldn't give him any trouble, who could be made submissive out of fear. He had just the candidate: he would abduct Carolina Kirksey. He had known from the first day he'd seen her that she was meant to play a part in his life. By now she had assumed a reality in his mind, a mutualness, as if they were actually acquainted, as if they were friends. Lovers . . . .

He even knew where she lived. He'd followed her that first day that he'd seen her in front of the market. Oh, he'd been very careful about it, she hadn't known he was watching her. He'd followed her to her house, had seen her go inside.

He knew where to find her.

Carolina had promised her mother that she would go to the Bertrams' just as soon as she cleaned up the kitchen after dinner.

"I wouldn't go at all if Con hadn't called this emergency meeting of the Village Council. I *could* miss it—"

"I'll be all right, Mom. Duchess is here. I'll lock the door. The Bertrams are just right next door. It's fine, it's fine."

"Well—"

"Bye, Mom."

Carolina loaded the dishwasher efficiently but without hurry. Mothers, she knew, worried needlessly. Admittedly, her own mother was not as bad as some, but lately she'd become practically hysterical on the subject of safety. It was silly. Windom, despite recent events, was basically safe. She knew everybody in the village. Besides, she had very powerful lungs. If anybody approached her, she'd just scream her head off. And Bert, right next door, would come running. That's the way it was in Windom, not like some awful big city where people didn't want to get involved. People in Windom *were* involved, like a family.

As she reached out to switch on the dishwasher, she paused. Before using the hot water on dishes, maybe she'd take a quick shower, then go over to the Bertrams'. That would still qualify as going quick-as-she-could, wouldn't it?

She dashed upstairs, put some music on the tape deck, and scampered into the bathroom. The hot water felt *fantastic* streaming down her body. She might as well wash her hair. Wouldn't take but a minute longer. Her mother actually meant don't wait for *hours* before going over to the Bertrams. She didn't mean *minutes*, and that's all it would take.

She reached for the shampoo.

Duchess, the middle-aged German shepherd, and the calico cat, Feather, had followed Carolina upstairs. The dog, by years of habit, trailed after Carolina for company; the more independent Feather stalked upstairs seeking a quiet place for an after-dinner snooze. With the solemn curiosity they reserved for the unfathomable antics of humans, the pair of animals watched as Carolina clattered back into the bedroom, her head fur wrapped in a towel. She dressed rapidly then, humming to herself, she plugged in the blow dryer and began waving it through her long golden hair.

The animals' attention shifted sharply at a quick small

sound that did not penetrate the roar of the hair dryer. Standing before the mirror, Carolina did not hear the noise which alerted the animals, but she did see their reflected reaction to it. Feather stopped in the midst of bathing herself and stared, one partially cleaned leg poised in the air. Duchess, a frozen statue, listened hard, her ears upright, her eyes worried.

Carolina turned off the blow dryer.

Carefully, Duchess rose to attention, listening.

Carolina reached out, holding her breath, and switched off the taped music, leaving an eerie silence to fill the house.

Duchess growled low, eyes intense, fur a-bristle.

Someone was downstairs.

Carolina hesitated, frightened as much by the tension in the room as by whatever might threaten downstairs. She trusted Duchess' instinctive ability to protect her, but it had never been tested. She was a fierce-looking dog, but had the affable personality of a big furry baby. Slowly, Carolina put down the hair dryer, unsure of what to do next.

Had she locked the front door after her mother left? She tried to recall the scene but it was too familiar—her mother's caution, her own casual agreement . . .

Had she locked the door? She didn't know.

Duchess had not wavered from her poised position and continued to growl low in her throat. There was nothing to do but go downstairs to investigate. Carolina couldn't stay up here, not knowing who lurked below.

"Come on, Duchess," she whispered. They crept to the landing and paused, listening to the silence below. It was just past dusk, and Carolina hadn't bothered to turn on the lamps which might have now dispelled shadows in corners. They started down the stairs, Carolina holding Duchess back by the collar with one hand, clinging in fear to the stair rail with the other.

Suddenly Duchess gave an angry full-throated bark and broke free of Carolina's grip.

Galvanized into action, Carolina followed, sprinting down

the stairs, yelling, "Get 'em, Duchess, go get 'em!" She rounded the corner into the entry hall.

The front door stood wide open.

Duchess was nowhere in sight.

Carolina hesitated, battling panic. Stay inside or go out? Where was the threat, where the way to safety?

Decisively she ran out through the front door and up the path to the gate. She had to get to the Bertrams' where there was love and help and an end to this nightmare.

And then, with a shock of terror, she felt strong arms encircle her.

First Tiffany, then Deb, now Carolina.

Somewhere, far away, she heard Duchess bark.

"Whoa! Hey, whoa! Carolina, calm down—"

Carolina broke free and looked into the astonished face of Deputy Lep Younger.

"Oh, Lep. Oh, thank God. I was so scared."

"Hey, it's okay, kid. What happened?"

"I thought somebody was in my house. The door was standing wide open."

"It was probably just the wind. You okay?"

"Yeah, I guess. What are you doing here?"

"Just driving by on patrol. I saw Duchess out in the road, thought maybe she'd gotten loose or something, so I stopped to check it out." He bent down to stroke the dog who had returned to stand, breathing hard, beside Carolina.

"Well, anyway, I'm glad it was you."

"Who did you think it was?"

"I don't know. With everything that's been happening, I was just scared. I thought there was somebody in the house."

"Oh, yeah? I'd better check things out."

"I'm going over to the Bertrams'. And, uh, I'd just as soon you didn't mention this to my mom, okay?"

Tommy was out of breath as he let himself in the front door. He'd outsmarted that damned dog by hiding in some bushes a few houses away from the Kirkseys'. He'd learned long ago not to be a moving target for pursuing animals. But he'd sure run like hell back to Crooked House after the dog had lost him.

He'd been there, in her house, heard her music, smelled her nearness. He closed his eyes, not in defeat, but in anticipation. He would get Carolina yet. Oh, yes.

Chapter 16

JANE, WHO HAD maintained an icy silence for some hours, was preparing for bed on the chaise in Allison's room. It was not easy to be silent and to ignore another person in such a small space, particularly when the ignored person is also an unwilling hostess.

Allison decided to rise above it. "Jane, I don't understand why you're so angry with me."

"You deliberately refused to support me against Tommy about picking up the mail. Mail is as important to me as geraniums are to Plum, and you sympathized with her. And," continued Jane, accurately reading astonishment in Allison's face at this display of petty jealousy, "it's a matter of principle."

"It would be," thought Allison. She said, "Oh, for God's sake, I didn't support you against Tommy because the basic issue was our survival. In any case, I hope that the villagers, who freely discuss every aspect of our lives, will notice and begin to wonder why we haven't collected our mail. It's a small hope, but we don't have very many to cling to. I did leave a note saying we're being held hostage on the checkout counter at the market."

"You did? Oh, Allison—"

She hated to dash the hope lighting up Jane's face, but she said flatly, "Obviously nobody found it."

"Oh."

"But our telephones are in the trunk of the car."

"So? They had to be somewhere, didn't they?"

"They're retrievable, Jane—if we cooperate. We have to

figure out a way to smuggle them into the house. Then when Tommy's asleep, we could phone the police."

"Plum's knitting bag!"

"What about it?" asked Allison.

"It's big enough to hide a telephone."

"Yes—if we could persuade Tommy to let Plum do some gardening, she could hide the bag somewhere near the garage. Then I'd find a way to retrieve it, put a phone in it, and leave the bag for Plum to bring back inside. Tommy's used to seeing her with that knitting bag so he wouldn't be suspicious."

"I don't know." It sounded too unwieldy a plan to Jane. She had another idea. "If only we could get that silly bomb away from him."

"Well, I don't know how we could do that. Except—"

"Except what?"

"Well, I've been thinking about poison. Just enough to make him sick. What do you think of that?"

"I think it's risky."

"Well, whatever we do, we're going to have to work together," said Allison wearily. "With the three of us against Tommy, we're still the underdogs."

It was much later when the lamp had been extinguished and the tide was well on the way out, leaving the ocean's roar muffled and distant, that Allison said in the darkness, "Jane, are you still awake?"

"Yes."

"I'm sorry about this morning. I had no right to say such a dreadful thing. We've been friends too long."

More silence. Then, "I'd like to tell you about Logan, Allison."

"There's no need."

"No, I want to."

"Shall I turn on the light?"

"No."

There was a pause so long that Allison thought Jane had drifted off to sleep.

"I married Logan Browne when I was young enough to believe that loving somebody was all that was needed to help them change. Did you ever make that mistake?"

"Yes." Allison's first husband had been a shameless womanizer, and she'd foolishly believed that all he needed to mend his ways was her love.

"When I met Logan I thought he was the most wonderful man on earth. He'd just finished his residency, and I saw him as a dedicated doctor who only wanted to heal human suffering. I believed that his coldness was a mask for shyness, and that if I showed him enough love and tenderness he'd be able to shed that mask and discover that he could be openly warm and loving to other people. I wonder now that I was ever so young and naive. Logan was an absolutely selfish man, devoid of feelings. Oh, he was a brilliant doctor, skilled and quick and highly regarded among his colleagues. If you're brilliant enough, people will overlook all sorts of faults. Logan Browne was a thoroughly rotten human being.

"Of course, he was wretchedly insecure. Any freshman in a basic psych class could make that diagnosis today. Back then, though, I just assumed it was all my fault that he behaved so badly, that he was so miserably unhappy with me. It just had to be my fault. And he played on that, constantly berating me for being stupid. And I knew no better than to believe him. He was a terrible man. I know that now as I could not then.

"I desperately wanted children. Logan was such a perverse man that simple awareness of what another person wanted was sufficient reason to withhold it, to deny it. He refused to even discuss having children.

"Eventually I met a man." Jane fell silent for a moment. "This is very difficult for me, Allison."

"You don't have to go on."

"No, I want to. I've held it in too long. I met a man who was all those things that Logan could never be. I fell in love with him and we had an affair." She gave a small laugh. "Such an old-fashioned word, affair. But things weren't like they are today. A married woman embarking on an affair invited scandal and censure. We were very discreet. Not very responsible, however, because I became pregnant. Logan knew the child couldn't possibly be his. He refused to give me a divorce and I broke off the affair. There was no thought of marrying the other man. Logan pretended to forgive all.

"After the birth of my son, Logan became increasingly abusive. At first he simply berated me privately, and in public. I took it, of course, believing that it was punishment I deserved for being adulterous. Another old-fashioned word—

"Then he raised the ante: he escalated the battle to physical abuse. Sometimes now when I read about battered women who stay with such abusive men, I am appalled that they think they deserve to be beaten. But *I* believed it. Even though in a corner of my mind, I recognized that Logan was sick, that nobody ever deserves such abuse, I stayed with him. I had my son to consider and I had no money of my own. I saw no choice but to stay.

"And then when my son was almost four, Logan, who'd simply ignored his existence up until then, suddenly turned his brutality onto my son. At first it was just angry words, then it became physical. And that's when my sanity finally reasserted itself. I might have been guilty and deserved punishment, but my son did not.

"The night of the burglary, Logan struck my son so hard that—that he knocked him unconscious. When I intervened, he beat me. He was a brutal, vicious monster. When it was over, he went downstairs. Resting, I suppose, from the energy he'd spent in beating a woman and a child. I was upstairs, trying to care for my son and myself, trying to figure out a way to get out of there. I'd made up my mind that I'd leave, even if I had to sell pencils on the street corner, I'd leave this man. He'd never touch my child again.

"After a while, I heard loud voices from downstairs. Then I heard Logan yell at me to bring the gun. I got it out of the drawer where he kept it. The gun was loaded, and I sometimes think that I knew the moment I touched that gun that I meant to kill Logan, that I'd have a better chance throwing myself on the mercy of a thief than with Logan.

"I went downstairs and it was all as Tommy described. There was this wretched-looking thief standing there— Tommy's father, as it turned out. I can see him still: a common-looking man, furtive, terrified. Logan was cursing at him and yelling like a madman. I cannot tell you how much I detested Logan. He'd beaten me, he'd beaten my son, and all I could think was: 'You'll never harm either of us again, you bastard.' And I pulled the trigger. I watched him fall and had no pity for him, no sorrow for what I'd done. He got exactly what he deserved. I looked him right in the eyes as I shot him and I felt absolutely free. I wished I'd killed him sooner, before he'd ever struck my child.

"And then, when I'd shot Logan, I looked at the burglar. He was scared out of his wits. I had no thought of killing him, of course. He'd done me no harm, he was a human being. Logan had ceased to be anything human to me.

"So it all happened quite as Tommy told it. Except that I never imagined that I wouldn't be accused and charged with Logan's murder. I didn't think of it as self-defense or insanity or blaming the killing on anyone else. The thief ran away and I just stood there, watching him go. I phoned the police and when they came and saw the forced entry, they made assumptions. I tried to tell them I'd shot Logan but they thought I was hysterical, I suppose. They thought the burglar had attacked both my son and me. I didn't tell them Logan had beaten us. I was too ashamed. There was such utter confusion, in fact, that it was days before I fully understood that I wasn't to be arrested for murder. If they'd charged Tommy's father, I'd have told them the truth, of course. I'm not a monster. But they never caught him and I never told anybody the truth, not even my son."

"My God, Jane, you've carried this with you all these years?"

"I've never regretted what I did, Allison. I'd do it again.

I've lived with it. That's been my penance. I will never forget it, but I do not regret it."

Allison lay awake a long time after Jane had fallen asleep. She'd never understood battered women, would never have imagined that someone like Jane could have been subjected to such treatment or would have submitted to it so meekly. Of the four husbands Allison had accumulated, she'd made two poor choices, but none had ever raised a hand to her, though doubtless some had been mightily tempted. No, no man had ever struck her and no one was going to. She'd never allowed any man to have power over her.

Tommy Weed.

What had she been thinking of to allow Tommy Weed to exert his power over her while she'd coddled herself as weak and old? Did she believe that she, like the battered young Jane, deserved such treatment just because she was vulnerable?

Hell, no, she didn't deserve it. She could wait for that man at the post office to discover their mail, wait for Chris Kirksey to put hints together and come up with the truth, but it might be a disastrously long wait. She—they—would have to exert their own personal power.

Allison's life had been full and difficult and rewarding. She had endured. She had come here to Windom, wanting nothing more complicated than to live quietly with her friends, listening to familiar music, reading favorite books, drinking good wine, gazing at the restful sea.

What right did Tommy Weed have to spoil all this? The nerve of him!

And her friends had earned their rest, too. Hadn't Plum raised four sons, endured the anguish of one's death, put up with the Judge and his cocky paternalism for all those years? Hadn't she cooked and sewn and volunteered and waited on people enough for one lifetime? Couldn't she be left to do that idiotic tatting that gave her such mysterious pleasure and to watch TV and rest her tired little feet?

And Jane. God knows, Jane had earned a rest. Carrying

around the awful secret of Logan Browne's death, raising
that son all by herself, working with those half-literate
engineers all those years. Wasn't it time for her to be left
alone with her journal, her poetry, her roots and berries?

Yes, no doubt that they'd all earned a rest, earned the quiet
of this lovely house. That's why Allison had brought them
all together in the first place. But that wasn't the way it was
to be. There was another challenge to be met. They could
give in to Tommy Weed but he'd just continue to use them,
possibly kill them. No, that was not going to happen. *They
were not going to give in.* Allison would see to that. She felt her
energy surging. They were going to triumph over Tommy.
And he thought he'd tangled with a bunch of pathetic old
ladies who'd let him run over them!

Allison's eyes closed as she headed for the splendid refresh-
ing sleep that comes when a course of action has been
determined.

She did not hear the back door open as Tommy walked out
into the night.

Chris Kirksey's first thought was that she would never in a
million years become accustomed to the alarming summons
of the telephone in the middle of the night.

"Chris? Sorry to wake you. Know who this is?"

"Lep." Nobody else would play Guess Who at two A.M.

"Yeah. Listen, there's been another one."

"Another one what?"

"Another attack. On the beach. Same area, around
Crooked House."

"Oh, God—who?"

"Candy Ann Lester. Tiffany Sims' roommate."

"How is she?"

"Roughed up pretty bad."

"Where are you now?"

"Dr. Woodring's office."

"I'll be right there." Chris started to hang up.

"Well, listen, Chris, we're about through here. I'll just
run Candy Ann on home. I can handle it."

"I'll meet you at her house."

"Thanks for the vote of confidence."

Chris hung up. "Creep," she muttered, reaching for her
jeans.

Tommy stretched out full length on Jane's bed. He was
fuzzily content with himself, or as near to contentment as he
could be. Most of the time Tommy felt thwarted by life. But
occasionally, as now, he swam in a sea of euphoria, believing
that finally he'd found the elusive thread of magic that would
set him on his way, free at last. He was like a gardener who
carefully tends a green plant, certain that this is the stunning
exhibit that will sweep all the prizes, bestowing fortune upon
him; when he displays it, however, he finds that all his effort
has gone into the cultivation of a commonplace dandelion.

Still he fantasizes. He plots, he plans.

"Things are going to turn out all right," he sang to
himself in a reassuring refrain. "I'm in a tight spot now but
there's a way out. Not tomorrow—that's too soon—but the
day after, I'll get out of here. And I'll figure out a way to take
Carolina with me. I'll lock those old ladies in their rooms,
but first I'm gonna take that Allison down a peg or two." His
fists curled involuntarily in anticipation. "Stuck up bitch,
lookin' down her nose at me, thinks she's better than me. I'll
show her a thing or two. I'll knock that high-and-mighty
look off her face."

He saw himself towering above Allison, striking her as
hard as he could—pounding the haughtiness out of her. He
could see her begging him for mercy, just as his mother had,
just as the others had.

Chapter 17

CANDY ANN LESTER looked awful. Her face was puffy, her clothing was torn, her hair disheveled. She was a large young woman, given to a fondness for sweets and french fries, for wearing jeans and sweaters stretched too snug on her large frame. Chris felt sorry for her; Candy Ann was too loud, too anxious to please, too pathetically eager to be loved.

Lep Younger hovered over Candy Ann like a worried rooster. "Look," he said to Chris, "I've already asked her about this—"

"I know it's difficult," Chris addressed the young woman gently, "but I need to know what happened."

"I already told Lep."

"I'd like you to tell me."

She told her story in quick jerky sentences. "I worked the late shift at Harbor Inn. It was after ten when I got done. I decided to walk home along the beach. I was tired. All of a sudden this guy came up behind me. He grabbed me and started hitting on me. I didn't see him. I don't know what he looked like. He just grabbed me, knocked me down and started hitting me. And then he tried to kiss me. He tried to pull my clothes off. I fought him and I guess he got scared. Anyway, he left. And that's all I know."

"You usually drive to work?"

"Yeah, but my car's not running, so I walked."

"Couldn't you get a ride home with someone?"

Candy Ann looked surprised. "I didn't ask anybody. I just thought I'd walk."

Chris took her through various parts of the story again but

Candy Ann added no details, answering in her unvarying staccato manner.

Thoughtfully, Chris gazed at the young woman huddled before her. Certainly people did things which contradicted common sense. There had been two attacks on women in the village yet Candy Ann decided to walk home along the beach alone at night, not even bothering to ask anyone for a ride. Maybe she just didn't think it could happen to her, even though her own roommate was one of the victims. Maybe she's not too bright. Or maybe she's working through some form of survivor's guilt by exposing herself to the kind of danger that got Tiffany killed. People do behave foolishly, understanding only in retrospect the dangers they'd exposed themselves to.

She asked aloud, "What did you do after he attacked you?"

"What do you mean?"

"You said you fought him, that he must have gotten scared because he ran off. Which direction did he run?"

"I don't know."

"What did you do after he left?"

"I went up toward the Seafarer."

"Then what?"

"I got to the main street and saw Lep's patrol car and flagged him down and told him what happened and he took me to Dr. Woodring's."

Chris glanced at her deputy.

"I searched the area while Doc Woodring was patching her up." He shrugged his broad shoulders. "I didn't see anybody."

Chris looked at the two of them. She was not satisfied. Not at all.

Allison offered to help Plum make breakfast and Plum, who was not one to hold grudges, saw this gesture as an extended olive branch and gave Allison a hug which was awkwardly returned.

"I'm so glad we're friends again."

"Listen, Plum, we don't have much time. I'm going to try to get Tommy to let you work outdoors with your flowers—"

"Oh!" Plum clasped her hands in childlike delight.

"And when you go outside, take that knitting bag of yours with you. Leave some of the yarn in it but just enough to cover up something about this big." She measured out a small phone.

"But why would I want my knitting bag outside when I work in the garden?"

"This is really important, Plum. Just do it, please. Take the bag outside and when Tommy's not looking, hide it by that blue bush."

"Hydrangea—"

"Whatever, hydrangea, by the garage. Or better still, if you can manage, just leave it some place in the garage, like you'd put it down and forgotten it. Don't hide it. I need to be able to find it quickly when I go out there."

"But—"

"He hid our telephones in the trunk of the car. I'm going to try to smuggle one of them back inside."

Plum looked at her friend admiringly. "Do you think you can do it?"

"We have to try. No one is going to come to our rescue, Plum. If we're to get out of this, it's up to us to do it ourselves."

Plum, primed by Allison, sighed heavily when they'd all settled in at the breakfast table. Methodically, Tommy unwrapped a Twinkie and bit into it; the white gooey filling spurted up like points of a mustache on either side of his mouth. Allison watched him reflectively. He opened a can of diet Coke and washed down the cake. He wolfed his food down, taking a big bite of cake, a gulp of Coke.

Plum sighed loudly again. "I feel so awful, cooped up here. I think I'll simply perish if I don't get outside."

"Nonsense, you won't perish."

"Yes, I will, too, Allison. And every time I think of my

gorgeous little flowers out there just *dying* for want of water, I feel absolutely *sick.* "

"You cannot be sick, Plum. That wouldn't do, you know. We must all stay healthy."

"That's all very well for you to say—you get to go out. I promise you, Allison, I shall simply *perish* if I don't get out and tend to my flowers." She turned her brimming, pleading eyes on Tommy.

"No point in appealing to him, Plum." Allison put a know-it-all edge to her voice. "He has said he won't allow you to go out and that's final."

Plum wailed and Allison said sharply, "Stop it this minute! Do you want to have another heart attack?" This was pure invention; Plum's heart, so far as Allison knew, was as healthy as it was loving.

"I don't care! At least that might get me out of here. I'd rather be in the hospital than stuck in this house another minute. I hope I do have another heart attack."

"Shut up, both of you." Tommy swigged down the last of his Coke and glowered at them. "You, Allison, you're the bossiest broad I ever saw. You, Lady Plum, I'm going to let you go out for ten minutes. I'm sick of hearing you gripe and cry. Ten minutes. I'll be watching every second, you hear me? You stay right where I can see you, understand?"

"Yes, oh, yes! I'll just pop into the garage for my hat and snips and—"

"No! No going into the garage."

"But I have to have my straw hat. I once had sunstroke—"

"All right, all right, for crissake. In and out. Then you stay where I can see you." He tapped the wine jug of gasoline which sat like a lethal centerpiece on the breakfast table.

"Oh, I promise I'll behave myself." Plum's childish delight was so real that Allison fervently hoped, watching her scuttle excitedly out the back door, that Plum wouldn't get so carried away that she'd forget her primary mission.

From the window over the kitchen sink, Allison watched

as Plum trotted happily toward the garage, knitting bag in hand. She reappeared almost at once, a floppy straw hat riding atop her white curls, pulling on bright pink gardening gloves. Allison let out a relieved sigh. Plum had left the knitting bag in the garage. She began happily snipping away at her flowers, a child let free.

Jane watched, too. Tommy was lounging against the back door where he could keep an eye on Plum's activities. He finished off his Coke, lit a cigarette, and after a moment flicked the ashes into the pull-tab hole of the soft drink can. Jane went to a drawer and got out a clean ashtray which she took to him.

"Here, use this. We recycle soda pop cans."

"Such goody-two-shoe citizens," Tommy sneered, but exchanged can for ashtray.

Jane rinsed out the Coke can and took it to the pantry where Plum kept neatly labeled sacks for recycling aluminum foil, cans, jars, and bottles. "Oh, these weren't washed properly. Tsk tsk." She took a wine jug and a jelly jar out of one of the sacks and bustled over to the sink.

Tommy, bored, smoked his cigarette and ignored the fluttery clatter of Jane's bottle washing. He desperately wanted to get away from here. He'd gladly leave these women to their fussing around food and flowers. It was all a great mystery to him anyway. His mother's idea of meal preparation had been to open a can of beans and dump them on a plate or to set a box of dry cereal on the table. She rarely even sat down at the kitchen table to eat with him, but would grudgingly set out the food. "Eat," she'd say and he'd sit down alone, spooning beans or corn flakes into his mouth. Sometimes she'd bring him a hamburger when she'd been out somewhere and she'd slap it it down on the table in its greasy waxed wrappings. "Eat," she'd say. And he'd eat the cold soggy mess, grateful that she had thought to bring him a treat.

And there'd been no flowers at their house, no plants, no shrubs, only a big maple tree that someone had planted years ago which had tap roots so deep that even their neglect could not destroy it. Once, at school, he'd been given some flower seeds. The teacher had instructed her students to plant them indoors and when the plants were strong, she said, they could set them outdoors to flourish and beautify their homes.

"Ask your mother for a little flower pot," she had said, displaying a new clay pot.

And Tommy had asked.

"What do you need that for? Does that bitch think I'm made outa money? No, you can't have it. Anyway, a boy planting flowers—that's sissy. What does she want to do, turn you into some kind of queer?"

Tommy had no idea what she meant, only that he wasn't going to get a clay pot for his flower seeds. When she left the house, he'd washed out a bean can and gone outside to dig up hard dry earth with a big tablespoon from the kitchen drawer. So carefully he'd planted the seeds and watered them, then put the can in a sunny spot on the window sill. Miraculously, a thin green leaf had sprouted. Quivering with excitement, he'd shown it to his mother.

"I told you I didn't want no boy of mine messin' around with stupid flowers," she'd yelled. "You'll grow up to be a queer if you keep up that sissy stuff. I think I'll go to that school and give that teacher of yours a piece of my mind."

Tommy knew she wouldn't, she'd never go near the school, had never been inside it, just sent him off there to get rid of him. He placated her by saying that he didn't want the dumb ol' plant anyway.

He hadn't thrown it away, but instead had hidden it in a drawer so that she wouldn't see it. He hadn't any idea why his mother thought the plant was harmful. Maybe if it grew and blossomed, and then he gave it to her, this beautiful flower he'd grown, maybe she'd be pleased and amazed at his accomplishment. But although he watered it every day, then tenderly replaced it in the drawer so she wouldn't find it, the early sprout withered and eventually yellowed, shriveled, and died. He didn't know why, except that this was the way of things. Dreams withered and died despite all you did to make them grow real.

He rapped angrily on the glass of the door and motioned Plum to come inside. Some people could make things grow, some people knew secret things that he would never know, some people had all the luck.

Plum had done her part. Now it was Allison's turn. She opened the refrigerator door and peered in.

"You'll be needing more cold beer soon, Mr. Weed. Shall I fetch the rest from the garage?" She'd deliberately left a case of the beer in the garage to provide an excuse to go out there.

"Naw."

Allison touched the extra car key she'd hidden in the pocket of her sweater. There was no hope of driving off in the car to get help, not while Tommy had that homemade bomb and hostages. The most she could hope for was to get out to the garage, remove a phone from the trunk of the Mercedes, pop it into the knitting bag, bring it inside to her room so they could call outside for help. Maybe she could call this very afternoon.

She shrugged with an elaborate show of indifference. "Suit yourself," she said to Tommy, "I'm too tired anyway." She touched a hand to her forehead and rubbed her back in a display of weariness.

Perversely, Tommy changed his mind, as she'd intended him to do. "Okay, go get it, but be quick about it."

"I'm an old lady, Mr. Weed. Quick is not something I do any more." She demonstrated this, shuffling out to the garage, fumbling with the entry door, pausing to grope for the light. Once out of Tommy's view, however, she moved quickly, whipping the car key out of her pocket and yanking open the lid of the trunk.

It was empty.

The telephones were gone.

She stared as thought she believed she might be overlooking them.

Tommy must have remembered the phones and hidden them elsewhere or even discarded them. She slammed the lid shut and looked around for something that might prove useful. Her eyes fell on a neat stack of a dozen bricks that were left over from one of Plum's gardening projects. She stuffed one into the knitting bag. It might be a useful weapon. She had to hurry now or Tommy would become suspicious. She picked up the case of beer and the knitting bag with the brick in it, grunting under the heavy load. She couldn't possibly carry all this. She wanted to weep at her own weakness.

No, she would not cry. Weeping would just keep her under Tommy's control. She lugged the stuff out the garage door, her old lady legs spraddled under the weight of her burden. She almost dropped the beer before she could deposit it on the kitchen table. She took the knitting bag and held it out toward Plum.

"Here, you forgot this. I declare, Plum, you're getting more forgetful every day."

Allison, exhilarated at her tiny victory, almost laughed as Plum's arm wavered comically under the unexpected weight of the brick in her yarn bag.

The urge to laugh died in her throat.

Tommy was standing behind her suddenly, his mouth close to her ear. "They weren't there, were they?"

"What do you mean?"

He pressed the knife to her throat, his yellow eyes glittering. "You know damned well what I mean, Allison baby. You went out there to find those telephones, didn't you? Didn't you?" The knife point pricked her skin, drawing a quick drop of blood. "Didn't you? *Admit it.*"

"Mr. Weed, you're hurting me. Please, take that knife away from my throat. It makes me very uneasy."

He glared at her. "Lady, if you don't take the goddamned

cake! I could cut you up into little pieces, don't you know that?"

"Yes, of course I do. I'm old, Mr. Weed, not stupid. At the moment, you need me. You've nothing to gain by hurting me."

"Not now, maybe. But things change. Remember that, Allison baby, things change." He smirked at her, enjoying himself. "You think I'm dirt, trash, don't you, high and mighty lady? You think I'm nothing. But you see, don't you, who's the smart one here? Who's the one who knew you musta found those phones when you went to the store and who had the foresight to hide them again? You know who's the smart one now, don't you?"

Allison, trembling, lowered her eyes.

"That's better. Just so we keep things straight between us, just so you remember who's in charge here. It's me, lady. And don't you forget it or you're dead." Tommy, calmed by Allison's display of submissiveness, smiled his crooked smile. "Okay. Now we got some more business to conduct." He sat down at the kitchen table, lounging insolently and, as if to emphasize his contempt for her weakness, he tossed the knife carelessly onto the table. "I want your jewelry. Gimme your rings."

She might have foreseen this demand. Don't risk your life for replaceable things, she told herself. Give them up. She hadn't known it would be so hard.

Tommy grinned, as if he could see her thoughts. He was innately shrewd in the ways of people. "Gimme your rings," he repeated.

Without speaking, Allison removed the glittery souvenirs from four trips to the altar. "I'd like to keep my wedding band from Mr. Moffitt."

"No."

She started to protest, then silently removed all the rings, placing them on the table before him. "You got anything else stashed there in your bedroom, anything I could use?"

"Trinkets, Mr. Weed. Costume jewelry." Would he

know the difference? It was hard to tell, he was such an odd combination of shrewdness and naiveté.

With a sudden and violent movement, Tommy was on his feet, the knife once more in his hand. "You're trying to thwart me, lady. I don't like it. I'll get you if you try to cross me. I'll get you good." The yellow eyes narrowed meanly. "I have a long, long memory for getting even and for getting back at people who thwart me. I know how to hurt people."

And this was true.

Chapter 18

GLORIA SNYDER'S summons to the chief of police was a timid one, heavily embossed with "if it's not too much trouble" and "if you don't mind." Chris drove to the hilltop house where Gloria, nervously waiting, opened the door before the bell pealed.

"Chris, it's about Deb. And—oh, dear—I don't know what Con will say about all this. He will be so angry. Oh, dear, maybe I shouldn't have called you."

"Well, I'm here, Gloria. Look, if it's something I should know, better to get it said and done with."

"That's what Con would think, but in this case—" Gloria's communication was strewn with abandoned thoughts and half-finished sentences. "He's going to be furious and I'm so embarrassed, I—"

"Nothing is so bad that it can't be said out loud, Gloria."

Gloria Snyder, who was by nature rigidly closed and fearfully aware of other people's opinions, doubted this. She'd have much preferred to pack up the family belongings and move to Alaska rather than do what she now had to do. She wrung her hands, hoping the gesture might help, found that it did not, and led Chris to the living room. Deb was again ensconced on the blue floral-patterned sofa, again surrounded by used tissues. This time she looked scared.

Chris sat on the sofa, diminishing the authority of her role by a smile and casual posture. Gloria perched on the edge of the love seat like a nervous canary.

"Tell Chris what you told me, Deb."

"It was all a lie," mumbled Deb into a wad of pink tissue.

"You weren't attacked?"

Deb shook her head and screwed up her mouth to hold back sobs.

Chris waited.

Gloria chirped, "Oh, dear."

"Can you tell me what happened, Deb?"

"I was staying over at Barbie's like I said. And they started teasing me, ganging up on me the way it always happens when three girls get together. Two are fine, but three get together and well, you know how it is, they pick on one. Well, I got sick and tired of being hassled. See, there's this concert in Portland and I can't go. My *parents* don't approve—" She shot a venomous glare at the mother whose medieval views were so obviously responsible for the situation. "Well, anyway, I had enough of it so I left. I first just thought I'd go home. And then I decided to walk on the beach and cool off, then maybe go back to Barbie's. I mean, they are my friends. Then as I was walking, I got to thinking how they'd be sorry if something really awful happened to me. Like, if I fell and broke my leg and lay on the beach in agony all night."

Deb paused to blow her nose and Chris, impressed by the drama if not by the plausibility of teenage imagination, said nothing. "Then I realized I was at that stretch of beach where Tiffany Sims got murdered and I was pretty scared, thinking that this was where it happened, that it could happen to me, too. And then I said to myself, well, why not pretend it *had* happened to me. I mean, who's to know? And it would make Barb and Steph suffer because they'd practically *driven* me out of the house and into danger. I just wanted to make them sorry for the way they treated me."

Ah, neatly done. Now her friends shared parental blame for the incident.

Deb continued, "Well, anyway, I tore my shirt—"

"A perfectly good thirty dollar shirt," lamented Gloria.

"It doesn't *matter*, Mother," said Deb in the tone of one who does not pay for her own clothes. "And I ripped a button off my pants." A look dared her mother to put a price tag on the trousers. "And I—I squeezed and pinched my own arms and neck and rubbed up my face and mussed my hair around to get it wet so it would look like somebody else had done it, had dragged me into the water and stuff. And I'm sorry! I know it was dumb."

"Yes, it was," agreed Chris.

"Oh, dear—"

"I'm glad you've told me the truth about it, Deb."

"Well, I *had* to. I mean, I heard this morning that Candy Ann Lester was attacked. I mean, if there's somebody really out there—well, he knows he didn't attack me, doesn't he? He might decide he may as well do it if he's being blamed for it anyway."

Ah, self-preservation is a good motivator for truth-telling.

"What's going to happen to her? I mean—" Gloria's voice was fearful.

"It can't be hushed up, you know. Not in this village."

"Will she be punished? I mean, legally charged with something like perjury?"

"No, she didn't commit perjury. And she didn't falsely accuse anyone of a crime. As for punishment—" All three of them knew that the worst punishment would be administered by village gossips. "Well, it will be rough for a while, then it will die down."

"I don't know what I'm going to tell Con."

"You'll tell Con the truth, Gloria. And he won't like it and he'll have to live through it, just as you and Deb will."

"It'll ruin him."

"No, it won't. It will certainly embarrass him, disappoint him, hurt him, infuriate him, but it will not ruin him." Chris got up to leave. "You might get some counseling, Deb, just to help you understand yourself a little better, to help you get through this."

"Counseling!" Deb scoffed.

"Con doesn't believe in counseling," explained Gloria repressively.

It figured.

"Daddy says we should learn to deal with our own problems without some shrink's interference."

"Well, he's about to have a chance to test out his theory, I'm afraid."

"Oh, dear—"

If Allison Moffitt had ever thought of adopting a symbol for herself she might have given strong consideration to the phoenix, that mythical bird which rose from its own ashes.

Although some might hold the opinion that her life had been primarily devoted to the acquisition and shedding of husbands, this jaded view of the woman was not accurate. She'd known triumph and defeat, she'd risked and failed, she'd tried and faltered. That was, in her view, what life was all about. You encountered some obstacle and you did the best you knew how with whatever brains and talent you possessed. Life was strewn with obstacles and the human task was to meet the challenge of overcoming them, or accepting them, or of learning something from them. Always, *always* you went on—learning, growing, gathering strength to meet the next challenge.

That Tommy had outwitted her with the telephones was a setback, an obstacle to be overcome. It was not the end of anything, it was not tragedy. Tragedy was giving up; not trying, tragedy was not having the strength or the courage to rise again from one's own ashes. Allison was not a tragic figure, never had been, never intended to be. Not now. Not at this stage of her life. Not she.

Think, Allison, think, she challenged herself.

Tommy had hidden the phones. Forget the phones. No. Forget *those* phones. There were other phones. There was one in the kitchen, but it was securely locked in the desk with the key tucked away somewhere on Tommy's detestable person. So forget the kitchen phone. Forget phoning for outside help.

What else could they do? They couldn't poison Tommy's

food. She had searched the medicine cabinet already. Spray Lysol disinfectant on his tuna fish? Hardly. Spray oven cleaner on him, like Mace? Possible, but it felt too risky to confront him so directly. They needed to disable him only temporarily, to slow him down.

She had some sleeping pills. Her doctor had prescribed them after J.P. Moffitt's death. Would they still be effective? Yes, probably—but how to administer them? Tommy was now so suspicious of his food that he ate nothing that was not canned or packaged.

And then it came to her.

The perfect way to get sleeping pills into Tommy's food.

"Allison, you know perfectly well poor Clovis was diabetic."

"And you know how to use a syringe?"

"Well, of course, I do."

"And I could just go into a drug store and buy one?"

"Yes, but why would you want to do that?"

Allison explained.

"Oh, I see. Except you don't need to buy a syringe because I already have one."

It seemed to Allison that a syringe was a strange keepsake.

"They're disposable, you know," explained Plum. "And I had a few left when poor Clovis passed away. And I never throw anything away that might be useful later on."

"Thank God."

"But I don't know how in the world you think you're going to get Tommy to hold still for an injection."

"We're not going to give Tommy an injection."

"Who then?"

"Not who—what. I'm going to put sleepers in Tommy's Twinkies."

Chapter 19

ONE OF CHRIS'S regrets about her working relationship
with Lep Younger was that they could not bounce ideas
between them in a comradely way. Lep had few ideas and a
paucity of imagination. And because he resented her superior
position, he behaved defensively and regarded sharing of
information as a giving in to her. Initially she had tried to
encourage him to be more forthcoming, had tried to support
his achievements, had tried to praise him whenever possible.
He took the praise for granted or regarded it as patronizing.
He did not take it in and never thought of returning it.
Moreover, if she did not praise him, he took this as unspoken
criticism. He was difficult.

Chris did not believe that it was worthwhile to make
monsters of other people. It discouraged keeping in touch
with reality and it tended to obscure personal responsibility.
In her own life, she checked and re-checked any tendency at
monster-making. The fact was, however, that occasionally
there were people who behaved badly, who were committed
to being hurtful or destructive. She concluded that Lep was
such a person.

It went beyond his unwillingness to work compatibly with
her, beyond his condescending attitude toward women,
beyond his belief that he could do her job better than she
herself did it.

Lep strutted around the village as a hero today, basking in
the sunshine of having come close to catching the predator of
village maidens. Was Chris jealous that he was in the
spotlight? Was she so blinded by her dislike of this boy-man

that she refused to give him credit when it was due? Was she merely being petty?

And why was she so suspicious?

She'd thought Deb Snyder's account of an attack was suspicious—and it *had* been a hoax. That certainly did not mean that Candy Ann's story was a hoax. Unlike Deb, Candy Ann had really been assaulted. Those bruises were certainly not faked or self-inflicted. And her rote recounting of the event did not render it false. Real life wasn't like movies, full of dialogue that actors mouthed from printed scripts. Ordinary people use ordinary language, often colorless, rarely dramatic. And ordinary people did foolish things like walking alone on the beach at night where someone had been murdered. Deb had done it; being there, in fact, had inspired the idea of the hoax. And now Candy Ann had done the same thing. The same thing. Yes, her story was identical to Deb Snyder's.

Chris traced the events reported by Lep, actively looking for holes, trying to pin down her suspicions. Yes, Candy Ann's car had been giving her trouble. The mechanic at the Shell station had confirmed this. Yes, it was unusual for Candy Ann to walk to work, but not particularly so, given that her car was impaired. It was surprising that Candy Ann hadn't even asked one of her co-workers for a ride home. But surprising things happened; perhaps she knew that no one was available to give her a lift, perhaps she was reluctant to ask favors. Aside from the fact that the women in the village were exhibiting unusual caution after the two attacks, Candy Ann was a sedentary person, not among the walkers, bikers, or joggers who daily paraded through village streets and along the beach seeking exercise. Yet she chose to walk home from work when she was admittedly tired. Still, people sometimes behaved uncharacteristically.

And it was not particularly curious that Lep had been patrolling the beach access road near the Seafarer. That was routine. It was a coincidence that he happened to be there right after the attack. Coincidence. He'd taken Candy Ann to Dr. Woodring's office after briefly reconnoitering the area, all according to procedure. He'd gone back to check the scene while Candy Ann was at the doctor's office. He had reported the attack to Chris. Nothing wrong with any of that. He'd taken Candy Ann home. His reluctance to have Chris question her was understandable, given that he was competitive and protective of his image. He wanted to make sure that any possible credit that might flow from the incident be attributed to him.

When she'd questioned Candy Ann, Chris had been aware of Lep's presence. He'd hovered. He wasn't a hoverer, wasn't sufficiently sensitive to concern himself with other people's feelings.

Candy Ann Lester.

Not a very appealing young woman, big and bovine as she was. And there was Lep, hovering over her as if she were a fragile figurine.

It didn't fit.

"It was Lep's idea to stage an attack on you, wasn't it?"

Candy Ann was a rainbow of bruises. She wore a hugely flowered muumuu which accentuated her bigness, and she sat with her none too clean feet curled up under her as if to shrink from Chris' accusation. For a long moment, she stared at her accuser, her eyes filled with such disbelief that Chris felt a pang of uncertainty. She'd made a guess and now she might be proved wrong—and worse, insensitive to an innocent victim.

Candy Ann dropped her gaze. "He said it would help catch the killer." For a person who could legally drive, drink, vote, defend her country, and get married, Candy Ann sounded woefully immature. She said defiantly, "He said you didn't know what you were doing, that you'd never catch the man who killed Tiffany."

"Well, he was half right. I haven't caught the killer. Not yet. When did he approach you with this scheme?"

"Yesterday. He came by, said he needed more information

about Tiff. We talked some and that's when he said you didn't know what you were doing on this case, that this maniac had attacked Conrad Snyder's daughter and that Con was real pissed. Lep said there'd be other attacks, that this was just the beginning. He said he had a plan but that you'd never go along with it. He asked if I'd help him, that we could fake another attack and Con would be so furious he'd see to it that you got fired and then they'd hire somebody who could find the killer."

Yes, thought Chris, Lep imagined he'd be hired to replace her. An absurd, childish scheme put forth by an absurd, childish man.

She looked at Candy Ann's pitifully unlovely face with its colorful bruises. "And Lep did that?"

"Lep did that. We went down on the beach. We made out for a while, you know, to get in the spirit of the thing."

"He roughed you up like that? You let him do that?"

"Yeah, I did."

"How could you allow that?" Chris wanted to shake some self-respect into this young woman.

"It wasn't so bad." Candy Ann touched her face gingerly, almost fondly.

"Dear God, she liked it," thought Chris. She felt sick.

"I thought I was helping. Besides, look at me—I'm stuck in this stupid village. I've got a waitress job that will last through the summer and then what? I don't work much more than half-time when the tourists leave, just as I'm needed. There's nothing to do here. The only friend I had was Tiff and she got killed. I'm nobody here. Lep is somebody. I thought maybe—"

What she thought was that if she connived with Lep Younger that he might like her, love her, take her away from all this, save her, end her loneliness, make her into a somebody. She was pathetic.

Candy Ann began to cry. "What's going to happen to me?"

"You're going to heal," said Chris gently.

Allison's doctor had given her some sleeping pills two years ago when her husband died. She'd never taken them because she did not believe in sleeping pills. It was her stern view that one did not sleep through bereavement, one faced it squarely, even if that meant wakeful, tearful, sleepless nights. Warring with this tough stance was her conservative nature that dictated a reluctance to part with anything that had cost money and might some day be useful. So she'd kept the pills with a kind of good news/bad news mentality: the bad news is that sleeping pills may be harmful to me; the good news is that I've got plenty of them.

She took the vial from the medicine cabinet. Chloral hydrate, 500 mg. She shook out a capsule and turned it over in her hand. She'd hoped the capsules would just pull apart like an over-the-counter cold remedy, exposing little beads of medication, but the contents here were more solid. How to get the stuff out and into the syringe?

She took a pair of manicure scissors from a leather kit and snipped off the end of a capsule. Inside was an amber-red oily liquid; this she squeezed out into her hand. She'd hoped for something colorless. Why couldn't that doctor have prescribed something transparent? Because, she answered herself, it likely never occurred to him that she'd want to sedate a murderer. She touched the end of the capsule to her tongue. Bitter. Well, it was obvious that she couldn't just squirt this stuff from the syringe into the Twinkie filling. It would have to go into one of those Pattie Pies. The pies were about the size of a big cookie and had a leathery looking crust. The filling was a congealed-looking mess of cornstarch, red food coloring, and artificial flavoring. Anyone who could eat such an abomination just might not notice the bitterness of another, more sinister, additive. Besides, she'd watched Tommy gobble his food. He did not savor what he put in his mouth, sometimes appeared hardly to chew it. It was worth the risk.

She had no idea how many pills it might take to immobilize Tommy. She didn't want to kill him, just slow him down. He probably wasn't used to sleeping pills, but then, she knew almost nothing of his habits. He might ingest all sorts of strange drugs. Well, she'd just have to guess. It probably wouldn't take too many, but how many were too many? She had no idea.

She shook two capsules out of the vial and looked at them. Might not be enough. She shook out two more. He was young. One more. What if she killed him? She shook out one more and shrugged. She'd just have to take a chance. She must equalize their strength, and one very groggy Tommy probably equalled one elderly Allison.

On Sunday, through hurried and whispered consultation, the women hatched their plan. By mid-afternoon they were ready to carry it out.

Carefully Allison wrapped six capsules into a tissue and took it into Jane's room. Each of them was to perform certain tasks. Allison's task was to determine the number of capsules and to get them to Jane, who would snip the ends and fill the syringe. And Plum would have to inject the sleepers into the Pattie Pie package.

Tommy habitually stationed himself in the living room in a chair strategically placed so that he could monitor the front and back doors and maintain a general sense of the where-abouts of the women. He believed that each woman in her own room was pretty well neutralized. If they made sustained contact, he yelled at them to break it up, like some insecure junior high school vice-principal applying the divide-and-conquer theory to his charges.

He heard Allison emerge from her room and walk down the hall to Jane's room. Although Tommy had comman-deered that bedroom, he allowed Jane to work there during the daytime, primarily because it kept her occupied and off his back. He knew she wrote poetry, and he'd dug through a desk drawer to look at it. Scribbled junk that didn't make any sense, was Tommy's opinion of it.

"Here are the slippers you were looking for, Jane. You left them in my room." Allison's voice floated down the hallway.

"Oh, thanks," responded Jane in a too-loud stagey tone.

Allison, who had a fine sense of the dramatic, cringed at Jane's patently fake delivery, and fled into the living room where Tommy sat. She selected a magazine and sat down in the wing chair she favored, elaborately ignoring him as if he were invisible. Tommy got up and turned on the television to a boxing match, hoping to annoy Allison who, unperturbed, began leafing through *Sunset* magazine.

Let her sit there looking superior, thought Tommy. What she didn't know was that he figured on leaving tonight when it got dark. He was gonna take that car and he was gonna leave, with money and Allison's fancy rings in his pocket. But first, he promised himself, he was gonna beat that smug look off Allison's puss.

There was something else that the old biddies didn't know. When he left, he was not going alone. He was going to take Carolina Kirksey with him. He knew where she lived, had been there, softly entering her house, hearing the music from her bedroom up above, sensing her perfumed presence. He was obsessed by her, fantasizing about her and how he might abduct her. The very word thrilled him. It sounded dashing and exciting to him. He would take her away and she would not only be his insurance policy against capture, she would be at his side, somebody he could care about. He'd give her Allison's fancy rings and she would learn to care about him. Why couldn't it happen? Stranger things did.

He looked up as Jane came down the hall and went into the kitchen.

"Now, where *is* that little white sack of mine? The one with *granola* in it? Oh, *here* it is," Jane sang. She emerged from the kitchen with a small white sack and swept off down the hallway.

Crazy broad, ate all that crunchy garbage. Tommy turned his attention back to the boxing match. He didn't care for boxing, it was too tame, not like real-life fighting. He liked the game shows where people got something for guessing right answers. He often knew the right answers on those programs. He wasn't stupid. He'd like to win some of those trips and prizes. Maybe someday he would.

Plum wafted into the living room bearing a little brass watering can with a long snout and began to water the African violets clustered on the entry table, then pattered off toward her own room. "I do declare, my little African violets are so thirsty today."

These women with their pattering and their nattering. They were driving Tommy nuts. He couldn't wait to get out of here. Just a matter of hours now. Anxiety mingled with excitement. He would make Lady Plum call up Carolina and get her to come over there on some pretext, he hadn't quite decided what, and when she got there, they'd leave, just drive off in the Mercedes, drive off into the sunset, like people in one of those fairy tales. Except that he'd have to tie Carolina up because, of course, she wouldn't want to go with him. He liked that idea. Now all he had to do was think of a pretext to lure Carolina over here.

Plum lost no time in collecting the white sack Jane had left just inside the bedroom. She trotted purposefully into the bathroom, locked the door, and removed a package of Pattie Pies and the filled syringe from the white sack. So far, Jane and Allison had done their parts. Now it was her turn. She felt nervous and dithery.

"Oh, dear, dear me—what if I'm the one to fail?" Her lips moved anxiously with her unvoiced fears.

The wrapping on the Pattie Pie package was clear and brittle. Why hadn't Jane brought two packages, just for good measure, just in case Plum broke through the wrapping on one? She had to be steady or she'd rip it. Tommy would never eat this thing if the package were ripped, not he, not as suspicious as he'd become. One false jab and the wrapper would tear.

Plum patted her face with her damp little fingers as if to

inspire courage in herself. She took a deep, trembly breath, picked up the syringe, and gave herself a quick pep talk.

"Now, Plum, you've done this a hundred times, you can surely do it once more." But her hands shook badly. She felt old and inept. She was just an old, fumbly woman, not good for a thing on earth. Tears welled up in her eyes and she thought of dear Clovis with his angel wings and his cigar.

"Hey, you—Lady Plum, what are you doing in there so long?" Tommy's voice at the bathroom door sounded so close that Plum almost dropped the Pattie Pie into the toilet.

"Really, Mr. Weed! You should be ashamed of yourself. We do have a right to our privacy and our dignity. Kindly respect that." Allison must have been standing right behind him, so clear was her voice. "Plum, just take your time and finish what you're doing."

Their footsteps moved away, but Allison's strong veiled admonition lingered. Tears and thoughts of Clovis were all very well, but what Plum needed now was some starch in her backbone. Dignity, yes, that was it. They'd all suffered indignity at the hands of Tommy and it was jolly well time to stand up and put a stop to this. She wouldn't let her friends down.

Cautiously she inserted the needle into the wrapping near the label. She drove it steadily through the crust and into the cherry filling. Skillfully she plunged in the sleeping potion, withdrew the needle cleanly, and let out a sigh of immense relief. She had done it.

She returned the Pattie Pie to the white sack and restored the syringe to the linen closet. There! Her part was nearly done. Now for the rest of it.

She emerged from the bathroom, deposited the white sack by the bedroom door and, lifting her voice in song, began watering her African violets.

"*In the sweet by and by . . .*" she sang.

Jane emerged from her room at this signal, walked down the hall, scooped up the white sack and took it to the kitchen.

She placed the Pattie Pie package on the counter with the others and carefully folded up the sack.

It would soon be time for dinner.

Carolina had experimented with a new recipe for baked halibut which she hoped would be as enticing as it had looked in the magazine picture. Tonight she wanted to make a special dinner for her mother. This was a matter of atonement, as Carolina was now convinced that she had left the door unlocked and that somebody had come into the house. Something dreadful might have happened to her.

Carolina had not told her mother of the incident, following some instinct that guided teenaged children to shield their parents from reality. She was guiltily aware of both her own flighty irresponsibility and of her vulnerability. She'd been badly shaken by the experience.

Like everyone else in Windom, Carolina had heard that the assaults on Deb Snyder and Candy Ann Lester were hoaxes. It hadn't surprised her about Deb, who liked to be the center of attention. She was, after all, stuck with those hideous parents. Mrs. Snyder, in Carolina's opinion, was always so scared of what other people thought, and Mr. Snyder was such a self-important little banty rooster of a man. Carolina had the breezy intolerance of youth toward most of her elders.

The matter of Candy Ann puzzled her greatly. How *could* she have allowed herself to be mistreated like that? Chris was furious about it, and about the hoax and Lep's part in it. Emily had dropped Carolina off at her mother's office yesterday, and even though the door was closed and Chris wasn't shouting, Carolina clearly heard the dressing down of Lep Younger: ". . . unprofessional . . . brutal . . . unconscionable . . . suspended until further notice . . ." Carolina didn't think her mother had overreacted about Lep. What he did was pretty terrible.

Carolina had been prepared for Lep to tell her mother about the incident of the intruder, but he had not. It

wouldn't have mattered, of course. She'd just have had to
face up to what she'd done. She supposed he felt that it
wasn't right to squeal on her, some sort of honor code
maybe. Or possibly he hadn't even thought of it. Confronta-
tions with her mother in that super-authoritative mode often
made one forget anything but self-preservation, as she herself
well knew.

At dinner, Chris complimented the halibut. She often paid
tribute to her cooking, which pleased Carolina, especially as
her mother was very specific in her praise instead of just
saying the food was good. Guilt made Carolina feel very
mellow toward her mother.

For dessert she served a peach and blueberry compote and
noted the flicker of disappointment on her mother's face.

"You wanted something really sweet, didn't you?" teased
Carolina. "Gooey chocolate brownies or deep-dish pie a la
mode?"

"You know my weakness for sweets."

"It's my job to keep you looking trim and eating right."

"You do it well." Chris smiled at their role reversal.

"I can't believe the stuff people eat. People who should
know better. Like that Mrs. Moffitt. All that money she's
got, and you know what Emily and I saw her buying at the
Gullway?"

"I can't imagine."

"Twinkies. And those gross Pattie Pies. Can you imagine?
A dozen packages she bought. Isn't that nauseating?"

"People's tastes vary. That's why there are thirty-two
flavors of ice cream."

"But she could buy anything she wanted, Mom. And
Pattie Pies—there is absolutely *no* nutritional value in them.
And baloney—yuck!"

"Well, maybe it's the other ladies at Mrs. Moffitt's house
who like that kind of food."

"Maybe, but I don't think so. One of them's a vegetarian,
Mr. Brixby says, a real health food person. And the other

one loves to cook. Why would anybody who loves to cook buy Pattie Pies?"

Chris had no idea.

"And, you know, the other weird thing is that Mrs. Moffitt was buying beer. Not just beer, but cheap beer. Generic. Two cases of it. And Mr. Brixby said that was a real shocker because when she first came here, Mrs. Moffitt was always asking him if he stocked those really expensive wines, which he does not. And now she's all of a sudden buying generic beer. That's so strange. Beer and junk food. I mean, you'd expect somebody young to eat like that, but—"

"Junk food?"

"I think maybe they're just getting senile, Mom. Not eating right and forgetting things. When Mrs. Bertram and I were in the post office yesterday, Mr. Rainwater asked if Mrs. Moffitt and her friends were out of town, thinking maybe Mr. Bertram might know, I guess. They haven't picked up their mail in nearly a week, he said, and he was having a hard time stuffing it all in their box because they get so much, and so many magazines and all. But Emily told him no, they were in town, we'd seen them in the Gullway this week. But Mr. Rainwater said it was sure funny that they hadn't picked up their mail because usually they never let a day go by that one of them doesn't come in for it."

Chris was thoughtful.

"Old people do weird things." Carolina spooned a plump blueberry into her mouth. "Like, there were those three telephones in Mrs. Moffitt's car. In the trunk of the car— isn't that weird?"

"Yes. Yes, it is."

"Anyway," concluded Carolina with the flippancy of the young, "I hope I never get old and weird like that. How's the compote?"

Plum had made a fruit compote for dessert also. Tommy had a beer and opened a fresh package of potato chips for his meal. The tuna fish was all gone, and his meal had not been filling. He had not been able to think of a way to abduct Carolina. And time was running out. He felt edgy.

"Would you like some fruit compote, Tommy?"

"No."

"Well, goodness sakes, Tommy, we're all eating it."

"I don't like fruit all weirded up in one bowl."

"You've still got some Pattie Pies. How about one of those, then?"

"They don't go with beer."

"I've made coffee."

"No. I don't know what you might have put in it."

"For heaven's sake, Mr. Weed, we're all drinking it. There is nothing wrong with the coffee."

"Then why are you so eager to have me drink some, Allison baby?"

"Mr. Weed, I don't care if you drink it or not. I merely think you're being unnecessarily suspicious. The coffee is fine."

"I like cream and sugar in it. You could have messed with the cream and sugar."

"That's true. We could have, but we didn't. I'm afraid you give us more credit for inventiveness than we're due."

Tommy considered this. His anxiety about leaving in a few hours had sharpened his appetite. He wanted some coffee and he wanted more to eat, as if his body were instructing him to eat now while food was available because soon it might become scarce.

"You get me a big mug and you fill it up with coffee and you put some sugar and cream in it and then you drink some, Allison baby. If you don't croak, I'll drink the rest."

"I don't care for sugar and cream in my coffee."

"I'm not asking you what you *care* for, lady. I'm telling you what to do."

Allison wanted desperately to keep the focus on the coffee. She took a mug from the cupboard and brought it to the table with the coffee carafe. Tommy watched her fill the cup, then measure out two spoons of sugar and pour in cream.

"More."

She poured in another dollop. Plum had made the coffee extra strong this evening. Allison drank a third of the mixture, then pushed the mug toward Tommy.

"As you can plainly see, I'm still breathing."

"Okay. Gimme one of them Pattie Pies. Raspberry."

Plum, who'd gone to fetch the Pattie Pie, looked flustered and Allison held her breath.

"Well, I don't think there's any raspberry left, Tommy," said Plum. "Just cherry. You like that." She brought the package to him.

He tore into it rapidly, and stuffed a huge bite into his mouth. Tommy didn't waste time relishing what he ate; food was for survival, not enjoyment. He chewed a chunk of Pattie Pie laced with sleepers and swallowed down a gulp of syrupy sweet coffee. He must have the stomach of a goat, thought Allison.

Plum began clearing the table, not trusting herself to watch Tommy's fascinating consumption. Allison and Jane couldn't take their eyes off him.

Tommy was licking the traces of bright red cherry from his fingers when the telephone rang. They froze, a quartet of statues, staring with fear or hope at the drop-leaf desk where, locked within, the telephone sang its insistent song.

"Who is it?"

"Why, Mr. Weed, how could we know who it is without answering?"

"It's probably my son," said Plum. "He calls me every Sunday evening about this time."

The phone trilled again.

"Tommy, Walter will believe it's odd if I don't answer. He'll be worried about me."

Tommy looked from one to another of the women, then extending the knife threateningly, he searched his jeans pocket for the key to the desk.

The phone trilled again, demanding that they answer.

Tommy found the key and threw it on the dining table.

"Okay, I'm gonna let you answer. Just don't say anything stupid, you hear me?"

"Oh, dear, I'm so nervous," said Plum, grasping the key with trembling fingers.

"Let me," said Allison. She was well-practiced with locks and keys. Quickly she opened the desk and Plum rushed forward.

The telephone stopped ringing in mid-trill, leaving them all staring at the perversely silent instrument.

"What the hell is going on here?" demanded Tommy.

"If that was my son, he'll call right back," said Plum.

Right on cue, the phone rang again.

Plum plucked up the phone as if it were a lifeline.

Tommy moved nearer and made a menacing gesture with the knife.

"Hello?"

"Mother? I rang just a minute ago and nobody answered. Must have dialed a wrong number where nobody was home."

"Really, dear?"

"Yes. Well, Mother, how are you?"

"I'm fine, Walter."

"Well, good, good." These weekly phone calls were often awkward for Walter Strawbridge, who loved his mother and strove to be a good son. Their accustomed pattern was for Plum to chatter while Walter made encouraging noises. He felt oddly adrift when the script varied. "I—uh—I read in the newspaper that you had some excitement there this week. Someone drowned in your area there, I believe."

"Yes, that's right."

"Nobody you knew though, I expect."

"No, we didn't know her."

Walter flailed around for another topic. "So are you still enjoying things there? Everything working out all right?"

"Oh, yes."

"Well, what have you been doing with yourself, Mother?"

"Oh, this and that. Cooking, needlework."

"You're not overexerting, are you?"

"Oh, no."

"Been walking on the beach?"

"Yes. No, not much lately, I mean."

"Is everything all right, Mother?"

Tommy, listening, pushed the knife toward Plum's throat.

"Yes, just fine, Walter. I—I'm a little tired tonight. I've been busy with my—my flowers all day."

"Now, Mother, don't overdo."

"No, I won't, dear. You—uh—you be sure and say hello to Clovis for me and you take care now, hear?"

"Say hello to—?"

"Yes, like I said, and I'll talk to you next week. I love you, son. Good night." Plum hung up the phone and collapsed into tears. It was all too much for her. The strain of Tommy's presence, the syringe in the Pattie Pie. It was too much, and then to hear Walter's sweet sane voice.

Jane led Plum to the table and patted her gently on the shoulder.

"Good girl—" Tommy smirked at Plum.

"Be quiet!" said Jane fiercely. "Just leave her alone. Can't you see how difficult that was for her to lie to her son that way? You standing there with a knife at her throat? Have you no feelings?"

The last question was rhetorical, as Jane knew when she asked it; Tommy Weed had spent the major part of his life suppressing his feelings in order to survive.

Plum continued to weep, Jane continued to comfort her with gentle patting, much as one would soothe a crying baby. Tommy stood tapping the knife against his palm, waiting for his adrenaline rush to subside. Allison watched him carefully. As far as she could tell the sleeping pills were having no effect on him at all. What if she'd woefully misjudged the dosage, assuring Tommy of nothing more than a good night's slumber?

The silence, save for Plum's weeping, had gone on for more than five minutes.

The phone rang again.

Allison, nearest it, immediately answered, imperiously staring down Tommy, whose adrenaline soared once more preparing him for action.

"This is Allison Moffitt."

"Allison? This is Walter Strawbridge. May I speak to Mother again?"

"I'm sorry, Walter, your mother isn't here. She and Jane just left for a—a piano concert in the village."

"Is everything all right? Mother sounded a little confused."

"Yes, Walter, everything is just fine."

"Well, the reason I called back is that Mother said—"

"Yes, I know, dear. She was in a hurry to leave for the concert. We're just fine. Don't you worry. And, Walter, please do give my love to Clovis." She hung up decisively.

Jane and Plum looked at Allison and she saw the hope in their eyes.

Tommy yawned.

Chapter 20

WALTER STRAWBRIDGE was thoroughly mystified.

When his mother had bade him greet his dead father, he at first thought he must have heard wrong. The longer he considered it, however, the more he worried. Was his mother getting senile? Did she have some dread degenerative disease with the symptoms only now being manifested? Had she taken a fall, perhaps, and loosened her memory function so that she'd quite forgotten that her husband, her beloved Clovis, was deceased?

And now here was Allison Moffitt tendering the same strange message. Surely disease or accidents did not simultaneously strike two people in the same household.

Walter Strawbridge was a man of logic, and he cast about for a rational explanation of irrational occurrences. Perhaps they'd eaten something that caused them to have memory lapses. Mercury poisoning from fish perhaps. Or, in the remodeling of Crooked House, some chemical might have been used in the paint or the varnish or the insulation that was affecting their collective brains. He'd read of such things, farfetched as they seemed.

Walter shook his head.

His intellect told him that something was wrong.

His gut feelings concurred.

For the fourth time in the space of a half hour, Walter Strawbridge reached for the telephone.

Allison felt exhilarated. The battle was about to be joined. The odious Tommy was going to get his comeuppance, she could feel it in her old bones. It would not be easy. They might get hurt. No matter; at least they were not going to be overrun by a sleazy young man who ought to have more respect for his elders.

Tommy had yawned three times already, and his eyes were beginning to look glazed. He knew something was wrong.

"There was something in that goddamned coffee, wasn't there?"

"No, Mr. Weed."

"You doped me!"

The women gazed at him mildly.

"Okay, you're in for it now." He brandished the knife. "Get in there, all of you, and sit down on that sofa in a row so I can see you. *Do it!*"

The women went into the living room and sat in a row on the sofa, like naughty school girls in the principal's office. Tommy grabbed the wine jug that was his bomb, the wick jerking as he lurched toward his hostages. He set the bomb down in the entryway, wanting it to be handy. He kept a menacing eye on the women as he moved.

"Okay, what did you give me?"

"Give you, Mr. Weed?"

"Don't play games with me, goddammit! I know you gave me something. I feel funny. I gotta think."

The women offered him no assistance.

"Okay, whatever it was, I'll find out. But I'm gonna lock you all up so I can think. Okay. Now, you—Lady Plum— you get up slow—"

Plum, who could get up no other way than slowly, rose to her feet, daintily smoothing down her frock.

"Now," he brandished the knife wildly, "you get your butt into your room."

Plum passed by Tommy with great dignity, then paused by her chair to pick up her knitting bag.

"What are you doing?" he screamed. Was ever a hostage-taker so vexed by his victims?

"I'm just getting my knitting bag."

"Git! Git! Git!" The veins in Tommy's neck stood out alarmingly.

"Please, Mr. Weed, don't shout so."

Tommy's patience snapped. "Shut up! Shut up!" he screamed at Allison. He rushed wildly at her, seeing his mother's face, the faces of all the women in his life who'd withheld, always withheld the only thing he'd ever yearned for from any of them, their love, their approval. He wanted to obliterate that face, his mother's face, Allison's face, all of them the same: remote, cold, unloving. He lifted the knife high.

Plum swung the knitting bag with the brick in it. Her aim was not quite accurate, but it deflected the knife in its descent toward Allison's face. Tommy, woozy and startled by the weight of the bag, reeled off-balance.

He dropped the butcher knife.

All Jane's T'ai Chi and yoga paid off in one glorious moment as she swooped to pluck the knife from the floor.

Plum and Allison rushed Tommy like twin tigresses, knocking him over and pinning his arms to the floor. Allison couldn't resist it. She trumpeted an ancient battle cry: "Once more unto the breach, dear friends . . ."

Tommy, who didn't know Henry V from Henry Weinhard, was not noticeably impressed. He might be drugged but he was a master of savage street fighting strategies. His arms pinned down, he used what resources were left. He thrashed his legs, kicking his heels wildly at Jane. He bit Allison's hand. She slapped his face, joyfully and hard.

Plum, dizzy with the triumph of her first assault with the knitting bag, was now on all fours trying to retrieve the bag for a second round. Unfortunately, her elevated rear end offered an irresistible target for Tommy's flailing feet, and he sent her reeling. Like a silent movie comedy team, Jane, still holding the knife, tripped over Plum's extended posterior and they rolled in a tangled heap.

Tommy escaped, though not easily, from Allison's raking

fingernails. It was all he could do to stand upright. He stumbled into the entryway where he'd left the bomb.

"You asked for this!" he screamed, uncorking the bottle. "Just remember as you go up in flames, it's your own fault!" His eyes on the women, he flicked his lighter, lit the wick, then lurched out the front door.

Allison, nearest the kitchen, stumbled toward the phone.

Frantically, she punched out 911 while the flames danced merrily up the wick toward the contents of the wine bottle.

Tommy didn't know whether he was laughing or crying as he stumbled away from Crooked House. Those stupid old ladies were going to be cinders in a matter of seconds when that flame hit the gasoline. They'd had their chance, damn them. He just wanted what he rightfully deserved. That's all he'd ever wanted.

He was befuddled. Got to get away before that place explodes, he thought.

The beach.

He headed for the stairs in the darkness.

Seconds to go before the house exploded.

He had to make it. He'd be safe on the beach.

All he'd ever wanted was to be safe. Damn, it was dark.

He reached the stairs.

One step, two. He stumbled over the soft dark thing that crouched there. He grabbed for the railing, missed, and pitched forward, tumbling into oblivion.

The last sound he ever heard was an agitated, recriminatory, "Meow!"

Chapter 21

THEY ALL ARRIVED together at Crooked House in a whirl of bright blinking lights: the fire truck, the paramedic unit, and Chris Kirksey.

Chris charged into the house, followed by Paul with a first-aid kit. The volunteer firefighters—Bert, Orin Brixby, and Mr. Rainwater among them—brought up the rear.

They all stopped, staring in profound wonderment.

Allison Nichols Ashmore Wyatt Moffitt came forward and said graciously, "I am so glad you've come." Her silk blouse was ripped at the sleeve, one earring was missing, her hair hung in her face, and with every movement pearls from a broken necklace skittered down her bosom and bounced onto the carpet.

Plum sat in a heap on the floor, a human pastiche of fluttering lace, knitting yarn, rumpled ripped dress, and bobbing white curls.

The hem of Jane's bright blue skirt sagged sadly, and her clashing green blouse hung daringly off one shoulder. She had the beginnings of what would blossom into a beauty of a black eye.

"Where is Tommy Weed?" asked Chris.

"He left," answered Jane. "He thought the house was going to explode. He may have headed for the beach."

Chris dispatched a deputy to search the area.

"Are you all right?" Chris's concern was real but she felt an acute impulse to smile: the old ladies looked so gloriously triumphant, resistance fighters who'd fought a good battle and were proud but exhausted.

Allison drew herself up regally and a few more pearls cascaded to the carpet. "Yes, we're quite all right now."

Chris asked, "Why did Tommy Weed think the house was going to explode?"

"He made a bomb," said Jane, pointing to it. "And he lit the fuse before he ran out."

Chris frowned at the burned rag in the wine jug. "But it didn't go off."

"It couldn't. I filled the jug with water and exchanged it for the one with gasoline in it one day in the kitchen. He never knew."

"I'll have to get statements from you, but I think that can wait till tomorrow. Are you sure you're all right? Should I have Dr. Woodring come up and take a look at you? Maybe give you something to help you sleep?"

Chris didn't understand why the three old ladies suddenly began to giggle.

Stepping out into the bright Monday morning sunshine, Orin Brixby left the Gullway Market under the reluctant supervision of his wife, Winnie Ruth, and nipped around the corner to Joe's Place for coffee. He'd seen Fudgie Pike leave a few minutes earlier and feared he might miss something. He wanted to be sure that the others knew it was his prompt observation of the change in shopping habits that had resulted in the discovery of Tommy Weed's whereabouts.

Mr. Rainwater from the post office was, as Orin had feared, taking undue credit for noticing that the ladies of Crooked House hadn't picked up their mail.

"Well," remarked Joe, who'd played no discernible role in the great unraveling, "I think the real star of the show was Chris Kirksey. She put it together that the old ladies were being held hostage."

"Those old ladies were pretty crafty, you got to admit that," insisted Fudgie, who always liked to call attention to smart women.

Nedry Jarvis, being a banker, liked to tidy up all the loose ends. "You know, I think it's just as well that Tommy Weed fell down those steps and broke his neck. The old ladies say he insisted the murder of Tiffany Sims was an accident. He probably would have plea-bargained that down to manslaughter and been out of jail in a few months." He shared with Conrad Snyder the dismal view that the criminal justice system was more criminal than just.

"Things do work out for the best." Joe offered his motto for consideration and generously refilled coffee cups.

"What's Lep going to do now?"

"After what he pulled, not even Con can support him. I'm betting he'll be fired, if he ain't already."

They all agreed that they'd never thought much of Lep Younger anyway.

The door opened and the pharmacist from around the corner came in for his morning coffee. "Well, what's new?"

They all clamored to tell him.

"You shoulda seen those three old ladies from up at Crooked House—"

Conrad Snyder was not a man to whom apology came easily. He did, however, possess a strong sense of duty, and he understood that he now had two servings of apology on his plate. He swallowed them both.

"Chris, I'm sorry that Deb lied about what happened to her." He was not one to equivocate in such matters, to embroider with euphemism. His daughter had not told a fib or stretched the truth. She had lied.

"People will understand in time, you know." Chris was not unsympathetic. They both knew that people would forgive Deb's behavior, but that they were not likely ever to forget it. The collective village memory was long.

"Yes, well, we'll just have to rise above it. Just go on."

"I think that's a healthy attitude."

"The other thing is about Lep Younger."

Chris was disinclined to let him easily off the hook on that one. "He has to go, Con."

"I know. I already told him. I fired him."

Chris nodded. "I want to select his replacement."

Conrad Snyder might be down, but he was far from out. "Well, now, I don't know about that, missy."

"Yes, you do." She looked at him steadily. And now that she had his attention, she added, "And Con, I don't like being called missy. It's demeaning."

He turned away. "I don't know what the world is coming to. Sassy women, acting uppity, making demands." He shook his head. "I liked it better when things were simple."

"Things never were simple, Con. Just different."

"Well, I don't like it and I'm giving you fair warning, missy—" He stopped himself but did not retract the word. "I'm giving you fair warning, I'll fight you to make things the way they ought to be."

Chris laughed. "Pull the wagons in a circle, Con. We've got a long battle ahead of us, you and I."

Jane had spent the morning ridding her room of the stench of Tommy Weed. She'd laundered the bed linens and sprayed the mattress with Lysol, emptied the ashtray and collected all the beer cans from under the bed. It felt good to restore order.

She would write in her journal later, write about the exhilaration she'd felt when she realized how easy it was to dupe Tommy by exchanging his lethal jug for a benign one filled with water. Her strength had been in her wits. She hadn't done too badly in her nimble grabbing of that knife either.

And later she would write a poem, extolling the virtues of people who worked together to fight evil. Maybe it could be allegorical. Individuals joining together to halt nuclear pro-liferation. That appealed to her. Yes, an allegory.

She stopped in the midst of dusting her desk.

Individuals, in and of themselves vulnerable, like Jane and her friends. But banding together, struggling for what was right, being certain that they could win over what threatened them all . . .

She put aside her dust rag and picked up her pen.

Plum filled the sink with hot soapy water and began to scrub down the kitchen. She liked things clean and shiny, and in the past week she'd not had the time she liked to devote to cleaning.

> *"I come to the garden alone,*
> *while the dew is still on the roses . . . "*

She raised her pleasantly reedy voice in song. As soon as she finished in the kitchen, she'd get right after those weeds in the flower beds and the rock garden. And tomorrow she must fertilize those poor geraniums.

This afternoon she would make a nice quiche. Spinach and cheese maybe. Jane would like that. And tomorrow night she'd broil a steak for Allison. They were such wonderful friends. They'd all been through so much together, not just this business with Tommy, but for so many years. Old friends, wonderful old friends . . . .

If they could combine their strength against Tommy, they could use that same cooperative spirit to live together here in this house. She was sure of it.

Poor Tommy, such a sad young man. Not like her sons. And oh, but hadn't Walter been wonderful to phone Chief Kirksey when he suspected something was wrong? Such a bright boy, her Walter.

As she wiped off the refrigerator door, she paused, listening for the mewling at the back door. And there he was, the black cat sitting on the step looking up at her with undisguised hope on its face.

"Why, hello there, kitty cat. Would you like some milk?" She poured some half-and-half generously into a plastic bowl.

"I'll have to get you some regular cat food the next time I go to the Gullway Market. But no tuna fish. Not for a while.

I don't believe I can even *look* at a can of tuna fish for a while
yet."

She bent over and stroked the cat's soft black fur. "I'll bet
you'd like to come inside, wouldn't you? All right, you can.
Allison is just going to have to get used to you, kitty cat. I live
here, too. I can have a pet if I want to."

The cat finished the milk and looked up at its benefactor
with enormous eyes.

"Such a nice little cat. Where have you been lately? Pity
you can't talk and tell me all about your little adventures . . ."

Allison's felt-tipped pen raced over the yellow legal pad.

—*Call Mr. Bertram to repair those stairs.*
—*Convince Jane to take driving lessons.*
—*Talk to Plum about That Cat.*
—*Call Chris Kirksey about donation to village police fund.*

Her pen ceased its scratching.

Oh, but they had all been magnificent last night. She
wanted to laugh with joy and weep with pride at the
recollection of their bravery. If they could work together like
that, they could surely live together in harmony. They were
strong women. They could do anything they put their minds
to.

She scribbled a word on the pad and, smiling, put exclama-
tion marks after it.

The word was: PHOENIX!!!

Bert had drawn up careful plans for the steps leading from
Crooked House down to the beach. Four steps, then a
landing, then four more steps. He thought it would work
nicely: a platform would make it easier for the ladies to
manage on these stairs.

He pounded a nail, then ran his hand carefully over the
board. Smooth as could be, nothing poking up to trip a
person.

He heard a familiar tapping.

"Mr. Bertram! Mr. Bertram!"

He looked up.

Allison Moffitt stood at the head of the stairs, whacking her cane against the railing. The wind caught at her elegant long sweater; her retrieved diamonds again twinkled on her fingers. Here she was again—Mrs. Moffitt supervising, questioning, demanding.

But there was a difference; she didn't look as frail as she had last autumn.

"Mr. Bertram!"

"Yes, ma'am?"

"This looks quite promising. Are you sure it's as wide as the specifications we discussed?" She whipped out her black leather notebook from her pocket.

"Well, you see, perception's a funny thing," he lectured. "Things a-building look weak and frail at a glance. But, finished and tested, they're solid, strong." He grinned up at her.

Allison Moffitt put away her black leather notebook, then gave him a small, not unfriendly nod. "Yes, Mr. Bertram," she agreed. "I do believe you're right."

About the Author

Mary Lou Bennett is a psychotherapist who also teaches at Oregon State University. With her professor husband and three children, she spent a sabbatical leave on Oregon's north coast where this book is set. Her articles have appeared in *Christian Science Monitor* and regional publications. She lives in Corvallis and is writing her second mystery novel.

About the Publisher

Perseverance Press publishes a new line of old-fashioned mysteries. Emphasis is on the classic whodunit, with no excessive gore, exploitive sex, or gratuitous violence.

#1 *Death Spiral, Murder at the Winter Olympics* $8.95
   by Meredith Phillips (1984)

> It's a cold war on ice as love and defection breed murder at the Winter Olympics. Who killed world champion skater Dima Kuznetsov, the "playboy of the Eastern world": old or new lovers, hockey right-wingers, jealous rivals, the KGB? Will skating sleuth Lesley Grey discover the murderer before she herself is hunted down?
>
> Reviews said: "fair-play without being easy to solve" *(Drood Review)*, "timely and topical" (Allen Hubin), "surprises, suspense, and a truly unusual murder method" (Marvin Lachman), "Olympic buffs and skating fans will appreciate the frequent chats about sports-lore and Squaw Valley history" *(Kirkus Reviews)*.
> Not recommended for under 14 years of age.

#2 *To Prove a Villain* $8.95
   by Guy M. Townsend (1985)

> No one has solved this mystery in five centuries: was King Richard III responsible for the smothering of his nephews, the little Princes, in the Tower of London?
> Now, a modern-day murderer stalks a quiet college town, claiming victims in the same way. When the beautiful chairman of the English department dies, John Forest, a young history professor beset by personal and romantic problems, must grapple with both mysteries. Then he learns he may be next on the killer's list . . .
>
> Reviews said: "a mystery set in academe that's wonderfully

free from pedantry or stuffiness (*ALA Booklist*), "a tight, fast-paced tale" (*Louisville Courier-Journal*), "nicely constructed and unfailingly interesting" (Jon L. Breen), "entertaining and illuminating" (Allen Hubin).

#3 *Play Melancholy Baby* $8.95
by John Daniel (1986)

Murder most Californian: murder *in* the hot tub, murder *with* the wine bottle, murder *by* . . . ?

When the obnoxious piano player is discovered floating face down with a fractured skull, no one has a Clue whodunit. Casey has his hands full already, what with his job (playing old songs in a new world) and new and old loves, not to mention thugs of various nationalities who keep popping up.

But the past won't stay dead. When he finds himself in hot water as prime suspect and/or next victim, he realizes it's time to play Sam Spade and dig up some clues. And all he knows for sure is that it wasn't Col. Mustard.

Reviews said: "readers will thoroughly enjoy the engaging first-person narrative, snappy dialogue, and references to popular music (*ALA Booklist*), "a mellow mystery with freshly drawn characters—more Woody Allen than Clint Eastwood" (Ralph B. Sipper), "well-written and invigorating" (*The Armchair Detective*), "I suggest that you 'linger awhile' with this one, for 'this is a lovely way to spend an evening'" (*Santa Barbara Magazine*).

Not recommended for under 14 years of age.

#4 *Chinese Restaurants Never Serve Breakfast* $8.95
by Roy Gilligan (1986)

The Monterey Peninsula art world is the background for private investigator Patrick Riordan's brush with death, as he stumbles across the nude, blood-covered body of a promising young painter in her Carmel cottage. On an easel nearby stands an oil painting which exactly depicts the murder scene—and which the artist has neglected to sign.

Riordan and his feisty sidekick Reiko chase clues from the galleries and boutiques of Carmel to bohemian studios in Big Sur to the moneyed world of Pebble Beach. The solution? An immutable condition, an inevitable conclusion: Chinese restaurants never serve breakfast.

Reviews said: "... characters are vivid and sharp ... the narrator has an engaging, naive charm. Gilligan also conveys the locale effectively" *(Publishers Weekly)*, "a likable sleuth and writing of assured irony" (Howard Lachtman), "fast-paced, detailed and skillful—worthy of a long series" *(Monterey Herald)*, "a likable work, notable for its well-realized Carmel setting, appealing characters, and unpretentiousness" *(The Armchair Detective)*.

#5 *Rattlesnakes and Roses* $8.95
by Joan Oppenheimer (1987)

When Kate Regal inherits a fabulous San Diego estate, family resentment turns to murder. She must learn that being tied to the past is as futile as trying to escape from it. The bonds of love, as well as hate and jealousy, are too strong to break—a lesson which puts Kate's life in jeopardy.

Reviews said: "well-turned-out romantic suspense" (Allen Hubin), "an appealing heroine, a good story, and the perfect book for a quiet Sunday" *(Union Jack)*, "unexpected plot turnings and rich, concise characterization ... Oppenheimer's natural dialogue and spare, vivid imagery make this an enjoyable, fast-moving story *(Southwest Book Review)*, "well-written, cleverly constructed, and entertaining; recommended *(Small Press)*.

#6 *Revolting Development* $8.95
by Lora Smith (1988)

#7 *Murder Once Done* $8.95
by Mary Lou Bennett (1988)

TO ORDER: Add $1.05 to retail price to cover shipping for each of these quality paperbacks, and send your check for $10.00 to:

Perseverance Press
P.O. Box 384
Menlo Park, CA 94026

California residents please add 6½% sales tax (58¢ per book).

There's an epidemic with 27 million victims. And no visible symptoms.

It's an epidemic of people who can't read.

Believe it or not, 27 million Americans are functionally illiterate, about one adult in five.

The solution to this problem is you... when you join the fight against illiteracy. So call the Coalition for Literacy at toll-free **1-800-228-8813** and volunteer.

**Volunteer
Against Illiteracy.
The only degree you need
is a degree of caring.**